THE EDGE OF MURDER

ALSO BY FRED LICHTENBERG

The Hank Reed Mystery Series

The Art of Murder

Murder on the Rocks

The Edge of Murder

Bridge to Murder

THE EDGE OF MURDER

A HANK REED MYSTERY, BOOK 3

FRED LICHTENBERG

ePublishingWorks!
love what you read.

June, 2021
ISBN: 978-1-64457-115-6

ePublishing Works!
644 Shrewsbury Commons Ave
Ste 249
Shrewsbury PA 17361
United States of America

www.epublishingworks.com
Phone: 866-846-5123

To my wife Sonia, with love and affection.

ONE

Nick Ross's life sucked.

Recent tragedies made it almost impossible for him to function as a psychologist. As far as his personal life, Nick was equally at a loss, drowning in his own misery.

Until last night.

Last night may very well have been the turning point in starting a healthy relationship. Nick sat at the base of his bed, his eyes closed, reliving the night before. There had been plenty of 'nights before,' but this one felt genuine, like it had a future.

It began when he'd decided to go to Courtney's, a popular haunt in downtown Fort Lauderdale, near the riverfront, about a half-mile from his condo. He wouldn't normally venture there on a Saturday night because of the loud music with crowds and couples—he'd be alone. What would people think of a guy sitting alone in a bar on a weekend?

Loser.

Nevertheless, he needed to push himself and join the world. Sure enough, when he arrived, Courtney's dimly lit interior was packed. He weaved around the crowd and found a seat closest to the end of the bar, far away from the loud, eighties rock band. Fortunately, Nick had learned to turn off the din when he needed to think.

That didn't work tonight, and before ordering a drink, the same dark thoughts resurfaced. His body tensed, and he was about to bolt, retreat to his comfort zone—though these days he didn't have one—when he felt a tap on his shoulder.

Nick stiffened. When he turned around, he was met with a warm, friendly smile that quickly turned to confusion.

"Sorry, I thought you were someone else."

Equally confused, Nick recovered. "That's okay, I get that a lot."

Nick could pass for many nationalities. He had that Mediterranean look: Italian, Greek, even Croatian. Standing at five-nine, he had straight brown, collar-length hair and striking hazel eyes. Nick Ross (Rossi before his grandfather landed on Ellis Island) was forty-two years old.

"Really?" she said. "Because from the back, you look like my brother-in-law. The height and haircut."

"Nah, just kidding," Nick said with a smile.

From behind, he heard the bartender say, "Hey, Doc, I haven't seen you in a while. What's your pleasure tonight?"

Nick turned to the bartender, a local college kid who worked weekends. Nick wondered how he'd respond to the question. He made it brief. "Been busy, Patrick. I'll have the usual, whisky neat."

"Sorry for bothering you," the woman said, and started to leave.

He turned back. "Wait, don't go." He pushed himself with a grin. "Can I buy you a drink, or are you meeting up with your brother-in-law?"

She smiled. "Sure, okay, sounds good. As far as my brother-in-law, I think he's on a business trip. I thought maybe he'd returned early. I'm Elizabeth, by the way." She extended her hand.

"Nick." He took her soft, warm hand. "What are you drinking, Elizabeth?" he added with a smile.

She turned to the bar, mulling over the colorful bottles of liquor on the shelves. "I don't really drink that much. I guess a glass of red wine." To the bartender. "A cabernet?"

"Sure, we have a house cab. Coming right up."

"I feel a little embarrassed," she started. "Please don't think that—misunderstanding was a pick-up line."

"If it was, it worked." By her looks, Nick took Elizabeth for a model. This place was full of them. Perfect skin, tiny waist, *the* look. He quickly dismissed his reason for coming to the bar—did he really have one? Though he admitted, meeting a beautiful woman with glistening strawberry-blonde hair, might be *too* much of a distraction.

When their drinks arrived, Nick held up his glass to toast. "What to, Elizabeth?"

"How about the meaning of life?" She smiled, and Nick was smitten.

He had been working on the 'meaning' for years.

"To finding the meaning." They clicked glasses.

Nick sat at the edge of the bed staring into the bedroom mirror, recounting the previous night until he felt Elizabeth's body moving slowly under the sheets, legs stretching, a toe nudging at the base of his back. He smiled to himself then turned to greet her.

Nick Ross was in love. And her name was Elizabeth. He turned to meet her tired eyes.

"Morning, sleepyhead."

Her long, athletic legs were probably still warm, exactly what he remembered from the night before. Warm and supple.

Was she the one? He'd kept asking himself each time they made love, which was two, maybe three times? He couldn't remember; he was too intoxicated with her.

What had begun as an ordinary day had turned into an evening of superlatives: perfect night, most beautiful woman, incredible sex.

"Hey," she said, then yawned. "You're up early. You a morning person? I think you mentioned that last night."

"I did, along with my whole life story. I hope I didn't bore you."

She stretched her arms. "Are you kidding? You're an interesting guy, Doctor Nick Ross. Growing up in Manhasset, Long Island, with loving parents, graduating from Columbia University, married…" She stopped. "Sorry."

He held off a moment. "Was married. And you said you were never married."

"I haven't met the right guy…yet. I'm working on it," she said with a hopeful smile.

Nick slid over and kissed her lips. The mix of her sweet redolent scent and sex was still present. She responded, and before long, they made love for the…who-cares time.

Their bodies exploded together as they held each other tightly, followed by soft, sweet kisses.

"I could get used to this," Nick said, still panting.

She sighed. "Me too, but we'd have to eat at some point."

"Oh, God, where are my manners? You must be hungry after all that work." He laughed.

"I'm starved. As I recall, we only had drinks last night."

Nick patted her on the rear end and sprang out of bed. "There's a deli an easy walk from here, and the food is to die for."

A yawn. "If they have take-out, I wouldn't mind staying here. I'll close my eyes for a while until you return, if that's okay."

"Sure." He got up to grab his clothes strewn about.

"Don't be long. I'm not through with you," she teased. "Food first."

"I'm on it." He slipped on his boat shoes.

"Oh, and would you mind picking up a paper? I'd like to check the local employment classifieds."

Elizabeth had mentioned she was an ER nurse but was looking to make a change. Any change.

"Sure." He pointed to the living room. "You can use the computer if you'd like. Be quicker. And as for a place to stay, *mi casa es su casa*." He caught himself, realizing he sounded too eager. "What I meant..."

"That's sweet, but I'm staying with my sister for a while."

"Right, you told me that."

Elizabeth turned serious. "I told you a lot about myself last night. Maybe too much..."

He walked around the bed. "Never too much. And as I recall, you moved to Florida from upstate New York to find a simpler life. And, you're an ER nurse."

"Close. I *was* in ER. I quit my job."

"Right, after you got burned out. See, I listened."

She brushed her hand across his cheek and smiled. "I thought I'd explore other avenues, but I'm not in any rush. I saved enough money to get by for a while. And like I said, I'm staying with my sister...and brother-in-law."

"Right. Thanks to him, that's how we met. Well, sort of."

"So how about you surprise me with something special? You got to know me well last night. Better than most people. What would I order for breakfast?"

He thought a moment. "You look like an eggs Benedict kinda gal."

"Close. Florentine."

"No kidding? Me too."

Elizabeth nodded. "I got to know you a lot, Nick Ross. And, you're more handsome from the back and front than my brother-in-law. But don't tell Billy that." She winked.

He zipped his mouth and was about to lean over and kiss her forehead when his cell rang. He glanced over at the dresser and scowled. "Kinda early." He picked it up but didn't recognize the caller. He was about to let it ride to voicemail but thought it might be a patient. Was that possible?

"Hello?" He waved at Elizabeth and walked into the next room.

"Nick Ross, you need to get out of your condo!" The voice was harsh and clipped. "Alone! You've got ten minutes."

A shiver shot down his spine.

"Who the hell is this?" His voice cracked.

The caller continued in the same threatening tone. "Don't jeopardize your life, friend. Get out while you can. There's a deli close by. I advise you to hang out for a while, have that second cup of coffee."

Nick rushed to the living room window and pulled back on the translucent curtains, his eyes surveying the street below. It was quiet, not even a passing car.

The guy knew his name, his phone number, and where he lived. And that he wasn't alone. What the hell was going on?

Nick kept his look below. Only one person knew his Sunday routine, but there was no way he would play this kind of mind game. Not now. Hadn't the bastard done enough?

His mind turned dark. "Chance put you up to this, right?"

"No, asshole, it wasn't Chance, whoever he is. You got *nine* minutes!" The line went dead.

Nick stood riveted in place. Had to be a crank. He wanted to stick around and wait for the caller to get back to him, laughing his ass off. But when two minutes passed with no call, he dialed back, only to get a blocked number.

Unsettled, he returned to the bedroom, where he found Elizabeth sitting up in bed. "Everything okay?"

He debated telling her about the disturbing call. They had a beautiful evening, so why screw it up with the likelihood it was a crank?

He feigned a smile. "Crank call. How about you come with me to the deli?" he proposed, fighting to keep his voice even.

Nick observed a forlorn look in her eyes, the first since they'd met. He checked his watch. *Four* minutes to vacate his condo or else.

"You go ahead, Nick. I'm kinda tired." She slid back down.

"Okay, but I'm gonna lock the door behind me, so don't open it under any circumstances. I'll let myself in."

"Seriously, Nick, I'll be fine."

He nodded. Could he take that risk? Should he?

"C'mon, I'm hungry already," she said rubbing her stomach and smiling.

He settled down, but then shot a glance at his clock. *This is crazy!*

Nick kissed Elizabeth on the forehead and left. His unit was on the third floor, but he skipped the elevator. When he reached the street, he surveyed his surroundings. He wasn't interested in the flowers and plants or the trees that lined the streets. He looked for something or someone out of place.

Screw this! He ran back upstairs. With less than a minute to go, he opened his door and quietly tiptoed into the bedroom. Elizabeth was asleep. He ran to the living room and sat on the sofa, but not before scooping out an eight-inch butcher's knife out of the kitchen drawer.

Seriously?

And waited. Crazy. After ten minutes, he took one more look

out the window. Satisfied all was clear, he took the elevator down to the street. Still unnerved, Nick's eyes darted about for strangers or unusual cars parked, but the street was still quiet, like it usually was this time on a Sunday morning. Even Mrs. Burke was on time, scooping up her poodle's poop.

Picking up his pace and glancing over his shoulder every few steps, he reached the New York Deli and was greeted by a few regulars who referred to him as Doc. He was the local shrink and had maintained a practice in the downtown area for the past ten years. In fact, a few of the regulars had been patients.

He stood behind three patrons on the take-out line waiting to order. He nervously checked his watch and tried to settle down. Was this a mistake? He looked around at happy faces enjoying their breakfast.

The food was definitely good here, he kept reminding himself. When he reached the counter, he was greeted by Kristi, the morning cashier and sometimes-graduate student.

"Hi Doc, the usual eggs Florentine?"

Nick smiled nervously. "Two orders today, Kristi," he rushed.

She threw a mischievous smile. "Hungry, are you?"

He wasn't in the mood for small talk and just nodded.

"Sure thing." She was about to put through the order when the owner, Jane Rosen, stepped out from the kitchen.

"Morning Doc, there was a call for you a few minutes ago. I guess he knew you were coming in today."

"For me?" His stomach tightened.

She nodded. "Right, said he was from your answering service. Something about an emergency, but the guy wouldn't leave a name. He said you would know him."

"An emergency?"

"Something about a former patient. I guess your service must know where you go for breakfast." Jane smiled. "Can't get away from anyone these days, can you?"

Nick's mouth dried up. His service hadn't called in...ages. Why hadn't they called *him* directly? And who was this *guy*?

"Then he said something strange, like be careful of what you eat. And who you dine with. 'Carnivores are deadly.' Sounded cryptic, but I guess you understand. This guy, he a vegetarian, Doc?" She smiled.

Nick ignored Jane's question. His answering service was made up only of women. And as far as he knew, none were vegetarians.

"The guy said to stick around and have an extra cup of coffee. And that he'd call you back when the patient was out of danger."

Nick dashed for the door.

"Hey, Doc," Kristi called out. "What about the eggs Florentine?"

TWO

With a nagging bad knee, Nick hobbled down the street, hoping his meniscus wouldn't tear. Slowing down at parked cars, he strained his eyes to get a glimpse inside the vehicles.

Nothing. He surveyed the street. Still nothing. Even Mrs. Burke and Tiger had returned home.

Taking a deep breath as he approached his condo, Nick entered the building. The elevator was waiting for him. Was he lucky?

Upstairs, he slipped the key in and unlocked the door.

"Elizabeth!"

No response. He rushed into the bedroom. Her clothes and purse were gone: no trace of Elizabeth existed. Nick gave his eyes a good rub, wondering if he had missed something. He hadn't, and felt a sense of dread.

He'd been warned. Yes, warned, but he believed the call was a prank, and now Elizabeth was gone.

He sat on the bed, stared at his twisted face in the mirror, and shook his head. Was she abducted? Or did she get cold feet? He hoped the second, though he would have sorely misjudged her.

He put his head in his hands. And what about the cryptic message from the deli? What patient?

What to do?

He pulled back the sheets from the bed. There were no traces of her on her side. He breathed in the sheets for her scent, searched for signs of...their sex. Nothing. Could he have imagined her?

A normal response was to call the police, but would he be overreacting? After all, it *was* possible Elizabeth had just decided to leave. Then why would she ask him to pick up the newspaper? A small nuance, perhaps, but...

Nick ran to his computer. He turned it on and watched it make its way to the screen setting, then checked for recent browser history. Nothing from today.

He raked his hair. How would he explain her sudden disappearance to the police? It was just over an hour since he'd left for the deli. "Officer, there was a blonde in my bed this morning, and she disappeared when I went out for eggs Florentine."

Not good, not good at all.

THREE

Fort Lauderdale

A day had passed since Elizabeth disappeared from Nick Ross's condo. He was beside himself, constantly checking the local news for crimes in his area. None suggested anything close to a missing person, or kidnapping or, God forbid, murder.

Walking aimlessly around his apartment, he stopped in the kitchen and removed a prescription pill bottle from a drawer. He popped a Xanax in his mouth to take the edge off, then went back inside, wondering if he had imagined Elizabeth. After all, there was nothing in his apartment to suggest she or anyone else had been there. He pushed himself to wait.

For what? Elizabeth to call and apologize? Sorry, *Nick, the sex was great, but I have to move on. Nothing personal.*

A ridiculous thought. What concerned him was the phone call. Or rather two. One at home, the other at the deli. Whoever called—probably the same person both times—wanted him out of the apartment. Why? To harm Elizabeth?

Nick didn't believe that, because when he returned from the

deli there were no signs of a break-in or a struggle. So, he held off going to the authorities for one more day.

Another thought. This one remained sensitive, and one Nick dare not address. He'd had romantic dreams about a very attractive patient. They felt life-like. Could…Elizabeth have been just a dream? He pushed the prospects of that theory back in his psychological drawer. Otherwise, going to the police would only invite an investigation. Perhaps, after discovering nothing, the cops would determine that the good shrink needed a shrink. Or worse…another reason to hold off going to the police.

Exhausted, Nick decided to call his mother, Angie. She'd been his rock and source of security and stability over the years. She was also a good listener, never judgmental. She knew about her son's former patient's suicide while under his care and believed that final act weighed heavily on his psyche. What she didn't know, because he never told her, was his desire for another patient—which he kept in check. It was perhaps this sacrosanct relationship that brought out romantic dreams. Hence Elizabeth.

His nervous finger punched in his mother's number.

"Nick, I was just thinking of you. How's my son today?"

"Okay, I guess."

"You guess? You don't know? The sun is shining. You should be outside—"

"I need your advice."

"Oh, sure. Does it have to do with a recipe?"

Nick rambled into the phone, letting the past few days take over his anxiety.

"Nick, hold on a moment. What's this about a missing woman?"

Nick continued at a slower pace, and when he finished, his mother said, "Son, I know you've been through a lot lately. Are you sure about what happened?" Her voice was tender.

"That she was here in my apartment? Yes, of course. You don't think I'm imagining her, do you?"

She held off a moment, and Nick realized his mother had doubts.

"Mom, I'm not crazy."

"I didn't say that, but between the past horrible events and your meds, maybe you had a dream. A good dream perhaps until…"

"It wasn't like that," he argued, trying to be convincing. "I would know if it was a dream. Elizabeth was real."

"Okay, I believe you. So, what do you want to do? Call the police? That might prove to be—"

"A mistake? I realize that, but I can't just sit around and do nothing."

"Let me think a moment. Okay, I have an idea. Call your cousin, JR. He's a New York City cop. I'm sure he's seen all kinds of crime. He'll help."

"Mom, JR's a homicide detective. He deals with murders. This is different."

"He's still a cop. I'm sure he'll figure it out without you having to go to the local authorities, at least for the time being. After all, there's nothing in your apartment to suggest anyone had been there besides you, including this Elizabeth woman. All I'm saying is JR is smart."

Nick knew his mother was concerned for his mental health and afraid he might be going off the deep end.

Was he?

FOUR

Nick hadn't spoken to his cousin, JR, in over a year. How would it look if he suddenly called and asked for advice? This advice? JR would probably think he had to listen to reason, that it was a great romantic evening and nothing more.

Still, he was desperate and finally built up courage to call. At first, it was about the family, which, since they were both only children, didn't amount to much conversation.

"Your mother is okay, right, Nick?"

"She's fine. She suggested I give you a call." He paused. "I know we don't communicate very often, and quite honestly, I feel weird calling you about something like this, but—"

"Nick, we're family. What's going on?"

With that, Nick ran through the incident as though his life depended on it.

"Nick, slow down. I'm not going anywhere. Start over and slowly."

"Sorry, I'm nervous. Okay, a woman disappeared from my condo yesterday morning after I received a crazy phone call."

"You mean poof, just like that?"

Nick went on about the call, the deli, and finally, Elizabeth disappearing when he returned.

"This is bad, JR. I've been debating whether to go to the police. I mean, what if…"

"Whoa, hold off a second. I know you're anxious to find out what happened to her, and it's been a little over twenty-four hours, but let's talk this through. Let's say this Elizabeth woman was snatched from your apartment; there would more than likely be signs of foul play. Are there any?"

Nick gave his place a quick look as though maybe the place had changed in minutes. "No, but…"

"Okay, that's good. Because if there was blood or a broken something or other, I'd definitely recommend calling the police."

"Elizabeth was real, JR, if that's what you're getting at."

"Nick, I'm not suggesting anything at this point. All I'm saying is there's probably a good reason she's gone. Maybe she got an emergency call and left in a hurry. Does she have your phone number?"

"We hadn't exchanged numbers at that point."

"Okay, fair enough."

"How did you and Elizabeth get back to your place?"

"She followed me home. Hold on." Nick raced for the living room window and shot a look below for the umpteenth time. "By car, but it's no longer here."

"Makes sense. I don't suppose you got her plate number?"

When Nick didn't respond, JR said, "Didn't think so. I mean, I wouldn't have either. Look, she probably just took off. These things happen. They call it cold feet."

"I know what they call it, JR, but it wasn't that!"

"Okay, take it easy. Is anything missing from your apartment?"

"She isn't like that," he defended.

"Humor me, Nick."

He crossed the room, opened a desk drawer, and pulled out a small, black leather jewelry box. He removed a couple of vintage watches, a gold coin, and a wedding band, which he gazed at for a moment then returned the items and shrugged. "Nothing is missing." He turned to his laptop on the table and pointed. "Including my computer."

Apparently, she isn't a thief. "You said you met her at Courtney's. Did anyone see you? Friends, I mean?"

Nick tried to remember, but he was so into Elizabeth. "A few, but we just waved."

"That's a start. Check with them, ask if they remember seeing Elizabeth. Or maybe they remember seeing her on another night. Hell, ask the bartender."

"What for? I told you she was there. They would just confirm that I was with her."

"Okay, just following through. Remember, I'm a cop."

"Sorry. At Courtney's, Elizabeth told me she was new to the area and was staying with her sister a few miles north. She was restless and decided to go out. She parked near Las Olas Boulevard, in the downtown area, and walked a bit. She stopped in front of Courtney's and looked inside. Something inside her head pushed her to go inside. When I mentioned that I decided to go out at the last minute, she called it kismet."

"Right, kismet. Maybe she just needed a place to sleep. It happens sometimes."

"Come on, JR, for a night of sex and little sleep? I don't think so. Besides, why would she go through the trouble of having someone call and threaten me? She could have left anytime. It's not like she was a prisoner. Hell, her sister lives near the place."

"Okay, good answer."

"And what about the crazy call at the deli? Makes no sense. I think she's in some kind of trouble. Maybe an ex-boyfriend is stalking her and found her here."

"And just happened to know your name and cell number? Doubt it, unless he works for the NSA?" JR laughed.

"Not funny."

"How about this? What if someone called Elizabeth *after* you left your place, and they worked up a scheme to call the deli?"

Nick sighed. "Again, for what reason? I told you nothing was taken."

JR thought a moment. "And this has never happened to you before?"

When Nick didn't reply, JR pressed, "Has it?"

"It's not what you think."

FIVE

Long Island, New York

My cell trilled, and I smiled at the number. JR Greco, my good friend and New York City's finest senior homicide detective.

"Hank, I'm calling to see if you've settled in yet."

"I just finished my first case. Less than six hours. I hope they're all this fast."

JR laughed. "I wouldn't count on it. So, you don't have a second gig lined up, I'm guessing."

"Not yet."

"Good, then I have one for you."

"Seriously?"

"Did you enjoy Fort Lauderdale when you took off to find a killer in Bimini?"

"You're kidding, right? I never left the terminal."

"Now's your chance. How about helping a cousin of mine? He's a nice guy, a shrink. Yes, we have one in the family." He chuckled. "Unlike John Hunter, in a prior case, he's alive. I promised him I'd find someone to help. You were the first to come to mind."

"How many private investigators do you know, JR?"

"Just you." A laugh. "I don't think it'll take too long. It's about a woman."

"Aren't they all?"

"I haven't seen my cousin in over a year. We aren't very close. I mean, I have nothing against the guy, but we're both very busy. And it's not like we live around the corner from each other. He's been living in Fort Lauderdale for years. What I'm saying is I can't vouch for the guy."

"Okay. You said something about a woman."

"Right. A woman he met at a bar went missing. They had sex, she stayed over, and then he went out to bring back breakfast, and when he returned, she'd disappeared."

"Maybe she got cold feet. It happens, you know."

"That's what I told him. Only, it's a bit more complicated. Like maybe he *thought* he met her and..."

"Delusional?"

"I didn't say that, but after I spoke to Nick, I called my aunt —they're very close. I told her about our conversation—within limits, and she admitted that Nick has been having nightmares recently. Sometimes he can't distinguish between them and reality. Again, this is my aunt talking. She told me about a few recent tragedies in his life, and quite frankly, if they happened to me, I would've lost my mind already. Anyway, she's concerned he might be losing his." He paused. "She's happy Nick contacted me and that I would help."

"Jesus, JR, it sounds like your cousin needs a shrink. I'm not a shrink."

"I know, but maybe you can look around, check with the bartender, anything that might help my cousin come to terms with this woman's disappearance, assuming she exists. Like I said, a quick visit might put my aunt at ease."

"Yeah, but if I come up with nothing, your cousin might not believe me. Then what?"

"I really don't know, but I told him to hold off calling the cops, at least,

until you had a chance to figure out what's going on. Make sense?"

"I agree," I said, rubbing my chin. I turned on the car heater and thought of Fort Lauderdale. *Hell, the temperature this time of year was probably in the seventies. Beats ten degrees in New York.*

"Good."

"I can fly down in a day or two."

"Thanks, he's expecting you tomorrow."

"You devil."

"Look at it as a paid vacation. Hell, if I were a PI, I'd go myself."

"Don't con me, JR. Okay, I'll need a bit more information. What's your cousin's name?"

"Nick Ross."

SIX

Nick insisted on picking me up at the Jet Blue terminal at Fort Lauderdale International. The place was busy, with cars and taxis dropping off and picking up passengers. I assumed most snowbirds had already arrived in December or earlier, because most passengers looked too young to be retired. I had texted Nick a photo of me—the best selfie I could find in my photo file, and he identified his car as a blue late-model Chevy Cruze.

When I reached the street, I removed my coat and greeted the late-morning sunshine. Welcome to Florida.

Perfect timing. Nick was just pulling up when I flagged him down with a wave. His passenger-side window was down, and he waved back. I guess the photo I texted did me justice. I tossed my carry-on in the back seat, then opened the front door.

"Hey," I said with a smile. "Hank Reed."

He shoved his thin hand my way and we shook quickly. "Nick Ross."

I jumped in and he took off like the terminal had the plague.

"Hope you had a pleasant flight," he said rather indifferently, as though he had more on his mind than my comfort. He kept his eyes on the cars in front as we passed a few terminal buildings. It reminded me of a procession.

"Not bad, but hey, it was worth leaving New York this time of year."

He continued driving without responding. When we reached the airport exit and turned north onto Federal Highway, he said, "Sorry, I hate airports."

I nodded. "Know what you mean. So, Nick, can I call you Nick?"

"Please do. And Hank is good?"

"I go by no other name. In the past, I went by Detective occasionally, but that seems like a lifetime ago."

"Good timing for me, you opening a PI business. I hope I did the right thing hiring you." He stopped. "Sorry, what I meant was maybe I should have gone to the police first." He half-turned my way and shrugged. "But JR assured me you were the best at what you do, so I'm taking a chance on delaying the inevitable."

"Which is?"

"Going to the police. Sorry, it's been very stressful."

"I totally get it, and, if at any time, you've had enough of my face, just tell me. I don't get hurt very easily. I'm sure after we discuss the events and look around, I'll be able to make a calculated decision as to how to proceed. I don't believe in staying beyond my worth. Okay?"

He nodded. "And as far as your fee, just let me know when you want to get paid."

"We'll discuss all that later. First, let's find Elizabeth," I encouraged him.

Nick nodded again, then wiped his forehead. He had a white-knuckle grip on the steering wheel and was clearly anxious. "Thanks." He checked the car clock. "It's lunchtime. Are you hungry?"

"Only if you are. I'd rather get started right away. How about we go to your place and I have a look around? I'll need as much information as possible regarding what happened, starting when you met Elizabeth. Describe her to me."

He sighed. "She's beautiful, model-like, with strawberry-blonde hair. I wish I had a picture."

I liked that he spoke of Elizabeth in the *present* tense. "That's okay for now."

Nick pulled up to his seven-story brick and mortar condo building and turned off the engine. "We're home." He attempted a smile, but I could see from his weary look that the past few days had taken a toll on him.

"Nice area."

Nick nodded, took a breath. "I'm glad you're here, Hank. It's been hell. I just want to find her, see that she's okay." And with that, he blurted out, in detail, the two crazy phone calls he received the morning of Elizabeth's disappearance.

Christ!

I didn't want to worry him, but I was freaked out. JR had only mentioned that Nick received two disturbing calls. Perhaps if he'd gone into detail, it might have scared me away. Hell, if I'd known, I would have drawn up a game plan, which, by the way, I didn't have.

Instead, I nodded calmly and suggested, "Let's have a look inside."

Nick owned a modest two-bedroom condo unit. His small living room was furnished with a mid-century leather sofa, two modern chairs and a rustic coffee table, on which a ten-inch bust of Sigmund Freud sat. Great conversation piece.

"I keep a copy of my patients' files there." He pointed to a metal cabinet in what appeared to be his second bedroom converted to an office. "I review an upcoming patient's therapy sessions, so it's convenient. I rent a small office in town for therapy sessions."

"So, your patients never come here?"

At first, Nick must have thought I had an ulterior motive for the question, and said, "You mean, do I have relations with my patients? I don't, never have. I hope that's cleared up." He frowned.

A sore spot. "I wasn't implying anything, so please don't take offense. I've been an investigator long enough to know all questions are on the table."

"Sorry, no offense. It's just…" He sputtered to a stop.

I'd hold that hesitation for later. "Let's go over the timeline again, starting with you leaving your unit and ending with Elizabeth's disappearance."

Nick closed his eyes momentarily and then brought me up to speed.

At least he was consistent. "Okay, let's stop a moment." I gazed inside his bedroom, which looked as though only one side had been slept in. I had noticed a sofa with a pillow and blanket lying on top in the living room. "You've been sleeping in there?" I thumbed to the room.

He turned and nodded. "I couldn't sleep in my bed. Plus, I was hoping there'd be evidence that Elizabeth was here. DNA, that sort of stuff." He looked in the bedroom and shook his head. "I mean, if there was foul play, you would notice immediately, right?"

Considering Nick was gone about an hour that morning, I would think so. But what if Elizabeth, after hearing a knock on the door, thinking Nick had forgotten his key, opened it, only to discover it wasn't him? She could have been snatched out, hence, no forced entry or signs of violence.

"Good thinking. I brought some tools of the trade with me," I said, holding up a hand and showing my carry-on. "Though, I can always get other stuff if needed."

"JR told me you were good, that you've worked together."

I smiled. "Don't tell your cousin, but he's a better detective than I am."

Nick sighed. "I wish we were closer. You know we're both only children. I moved to Fort Lauderdale years ago, and JR stayed in New York. Seems we never found time for each other. Strange, how we connected through…"

A possible crime? I nodded.

"I haven't reserved a hotel room for you yet, but we can do that now. The Riverside Hotel on Las Olas Boulevard is only a few blocks from here."

"I'm good here." I thumbed to the second bedroom/office. "If that's okay with you."

He shrugged. "Sure."

My reason had more to do with logistics than comfort. I wanted to be around twenty-four-seven.

"You can use my car anytime you need it."

"Thanks." I surveyed the living room. "Has anyone been here since Elizabeth left?"

He shook his head. "I didn't want to taint the apartment just in case."

I nodded, then removed a pair of latex gloves from my carry-on and entered the bedroom. Standing at the foot of the bed, I noticed one side of the bed was smoothed out as though it hadn't been slept in. That confirmed what I had observed earlier. The other side, I presumed, was where Nick had slept.

Nick said, "I left it the way I found it when I returned from the deli."

A pillow on his side leaned upright against the headboard, as though he'd been sitting up.

"The pillow's position looks like you might have been reading." I glanced over and shrugged.

Nick thought a moment. "That night, after we were together, and Elizabeth had fallen asleep, I sat up and watched her lie there. She was so relaxed, the rhythm of her breathing, I could almost detect a smile. Her hair draped over one eye. I was smitten. Still am. Is that weird? I mean, watching her while she slept?"

I thought about my past life with Susan. In the beginning of our marriage, I enjoyed watching her sleep. "Like you said, you were smitten."

"She was real, Hank. I wasn't imagining or dreaming. I sense JR and my mother suspect Elizabeth was probably an illusion, and I'll admit, in the past few months, I've had dreams and nightmares. But I was always able to tell the difference afterward between reality and illusion."

Until now, maybe. "That's why I'm here. If Elizabeth *was* here, we'll soon find out." Off the top of my head, I rattled off a few sources to pursue.

My assurances seemed to put him at ease, and he nodded with a smile. "Thanks."

I pulled back on Elizabeth's side of the bed. The pillow and sheets looked fresh, no wrinkles. I sniffed around, which I don't get a kick out of, and smelled fresh-scented sheets, as though they just came out of the dryer. I looked up at Nick. "Don't ask."

On Nick's side, the same fragrance was present. I held off telling him it appeared no one had slept in the bed. "How many sets of white sheets do you have?"

"Huh?"

"Just curious."

He walked into his closet and then stuck his head out. "Three, two are in here."

"Interesting."

"What?"

"Sniff the sheets. Tell me what you smell." I watched him whiff both sides and when he finished, he glanced over at me. "Fresh. That's impossible. I mean, even if I slept alone, you'd get my scent. Right?"

He had me. "True." I looked inside his living room and took in the blanket and pillow again. Maybe not. "Where do you do laundry?"

He pointed to a closet. "In there. Stackable."

I walked over and surveyed inside. Nick had a few soiled garments in a plastic laundry basket. I still had my latex gloves on and fingered the items. No sheets. That meant either he was confused about this Elizabeth or *she* carried around her own set of sheets.

Unlikely.

I wanted to believe my client, but so far, everything pointed to Elizabeth being a no-show.

I popped my head out. "No sheets. You said she arrived by car and parked out front."

"Right, across the street. You don't think she went into her car and brought back sheets, do you? I mean, why?"

Exactly. Why? I walked over to the window. A few cars were parked against the curb. "Tell me again: how long were you gone that morning?" I asked, watching the street.

"I don't know, around an hour."

Again, consistent. Enough time to exchange sheets. But why?

I turned to Nick. "And those sheets inside are definitely yours?"

He shrugged. "How could they not be?" He started for the bed then stopped. "Should I check without gloves?"

Smart thinking. "Here, let me." I pulled up the corners, looking for a label. There weren't any. The sheets were white, cotton and queen-sized. I then went back to his closet and examined one of the other sets. Same, no label.

Nick paced the room, then stopped in front of me. His lips tremored slightly. "You don't believe me."

It wasn't a question. "Look, Nick, I want to. Let's go over this timeline one more time."

He shook his head and closed his eyes. "Not again."

"Humor me."

He glanced down at the bed, then to me. "Like I told you, I met Elizabeth at Courtney's Saturday night. We had a few drinks. She had the house cabernet. I drank whisky neat. We talked about life for a few hours…"

I held up a hand. "Okay, good. Did you go back to Courtney's and ask the bartender if he remembers seeing you with a woman Saturday night?"

It looked like a lightbulb went off. "No. I guess I should have."

"Not a problem. We can do that later."

He closed his eyes momentarily. "The place was packed. Elizabeth needed to use the ladies' room, so I met her outside. She then followed me here in a red Mustang. And no, I didn't get a license plate number."

He was obviously frustrated by my questioning.

I continued anyway. "She parked out front?"

"Right."

"Okay. You also saw a few friends at Courtney's. You waved and they waved back."

"Correct."

"Did you call them afterward and ask if you were with a woman?"

He huffed. "No."

Nick was batting .200 in my book, not enough to prove she'd been in his condo. "We need to connect your trip from the bar back to your place. And like you said, none of the neighbors saw you with Elizabeth."

"It was late."

"Still."

"Maybe I should go to the police."

"Is that what you want, Nick? It's your choice."

He licked his dry lips. "I just want answers, and JR promised you'd get them."

My buddy had put too much faith in me. I had asked JR to run a check of crimes near Nick's area between Saturday night through Monday. He hadn't found any that would fit my suspicions. A few robberies and an assault. I wanted to tell Nick for the third time that Elizabeth probably got cold feet and left, but what bothered me were the threatening phone calls.

And the sheets? I doubted anyone had slept in the bed. I sat down on a small wooden chair facing the bed and pondered. My eyes drifted from the bed to the dark bamboo floor. I blinked, my eyes holding steady on a small dark spot just outside the bed frame. I got on my knees and approached it. I looked down and, with my right gloved hand, rubbed a dry spot.

Blood stain?

SEVEN

My cell phone came alive, and I told Nick I needed to take the call. I walked into the living room and recognized the familiar number, my former boss, Jimmy Stanton.

"Please tell me you have the kidnappers in custody," I pleaded, my voice racing.

"Hello to you, too, Hank. Yes, the reason for my call. I felt I owed you, given your quick response and success. Though, next time, if there is one, call the Feds before getting directly involved."

I smiled to myself. Stanton's way of complimenting me.

"Anyway, it wasn't difficult. When we arrived at Mervin Scott's mother's house, he and his fiancée were counting their ransom money on the living room floor and celebrating with chips and beer." He chortled. "They never had a chance to spend a dime."

"Oh, they'll be spending *time* for sure. Nice job," I quipped, upbeat that Stanton had the kidnappers in custody.

After a pause, Stanton said, "I owe you one, Hank, but don't use your gift card too quickly. You just started your PI business."

"I'll remember that, Boss. And the kid, how's he doing?"

"Better, now that he's home with his family, and the perps are in jail. Anyway, I just wanted to say thanks."

Relieved, I dropped into a deep black leather armchair facing the afternoon sun, the warmth soothing my pale face. I wondered whether I'd have time to enjoy some.

"This damn cold weather is killing me," Stanton complained, frustration breaking through.

I blinked into the sun. "Not here in Fort Lauderdale."

"You bastard! Another case?"

I glanced back at Nick, who was on his computer. "Missing person, I think."

"You think?"

I lowered my voice. "I'm hoping it's not foul play."

After hanging up with Stanton, I thought about the dark stain on Nick's bedroom floor. I didn't want to jump to conclusions. For all I knew, it could be wine, which would make sense *had* I seen wine glasses nearby.

Nick popped his head inside the room. "Everything okay?" he asked, interrupting my thoughts. "I mean with the call."

I nodded. "It was about a case I just finished."

He stepped in front of me, blocking out the sun. "How did it turn out, if you don't mind me asking?"

"We nabbed the couple, so I'd say it was a very good day for justice." I smiled with satisfaction.

He returned the smile. "Sounds like you might have a good track record." His body appeared to slacken.

Nick must think I was a miracle worker.

Keeping eye contact, I said, "Before Elizabeth, when was the last time you entertained a woman in your apartment? I mean, besides your mom."

He was quick to answer. "Never. Quite honestly, after all that's happened to me, I wasn't ready to date."

"Until now."

He tightened his lips and nodded. "Meeting Elizabeth was really a coincidence. If she hadn't gone to Courtney's that night…" He shrugged. "She's special. I hadn't felt alive like I did that night in a very long time. That's why I have to find her." He paused, looked as though he was about to cry. "I know what you must be thinking. Crazy shrink. But I'm telling you, Hank: Elizabeth was no mirage."

I really wanted to believe him and would continue supporting his insistence, unless my investigation suggested otherwise. If she was real, her disappearance meant she either wasn't into Nick, or, if she was, someone else wasn't about to let that relationship continue.

"How long have you lived here?"

"About three months. Soon after my wife died. We were living in an apartment, but after the accident, I had to move. Too many memories." He sighed.

JR never mentioned an accident.

Nick must have noticed confusion on my face.

"My wife died in a car accident. We were going to get a divorce…"

As I waited for Nick to continue, I could see rage in his eyes. "She'd been cheating on me for…I don't know how long, with my best friend." He wiped his mouth, tightened a fist. "The bastards."

Where did that come from?

Since meeting Nick, I hadn't seen him this openly hostile, so his sudden outburst was raw, and made me concerned. I could tell he wasn't over *her* by a long shot.

"Sorry," he apologized, wiping an eye. "Every time I think about them, I get a little crazy."

I waved a hand. "I get it, believe me."

"It happened to you?" Nick almost sounded relieved, as

though he wasn't the only schmuck humiliated.

I wasn't about to compare war stories. "Long story."

He fidgeted with his hands, then got up and left the room. He returned with two bottles of Peroni beer, which I loved. Handing me one, he lifted his beer bottle.

"To finding Elizabeth."

We clicked bottles. I took a much-needed gulp, then watched him chug his down.

Nick looked bewildered, perhaps wondering whether his wife's infidelity and Elizabeth missing were somehow connected, as though he was responsible. A long shot, maybe. He was the shrink, not me. But his animosity toward his ex may have set off his urgency to find Elizabeth, bring her back, and make everything great again. Assuming there was an Elizabeth.

I polished off my beer, and with no coaster in sight, kept the bottle in my hand. After a few moments, I said, "While examining the bedroom, I noticed a dark stain on the floor."

His head shot up. "Stain? Where?"

"Left side of the bed near the metal leg. It's small, but…"

Nick leaped out of his chair, dropped the beer bottle on the coffee table, and dashed for the bedroom. I left mine next to his, and when I joined him, Nick was already on his knees giving the stain a good rub with his hand. After a few more rubs, he gave up. "I've never seen this before," he said, glancing up at me.

He sounded sincere.

"Think it's blood? I mean, it could be anything."

"Were you drinking wine in here recently?"

"No."

"Not last night," I pushed.

"No," he repeated.

"Okay, it needs to be determined. And even if it is blood, there might be a legitimate explanation. You said Elizabeth was sleeping on this side, right?"

Nick scowled. "I hope you're not suggesting anything on my part. It can't be hers. I mean, how would it get there?"

Innocently or through an act of violence. I shrugged. "We need to find out."

A slight twinge came from one side of his face. Still on his knees, he said, "If you think we should."

I most certainly did.

"Do we call the police?" he asked, his voice flat.

"I have someone else in mind."

EIGHT

JR answered on the first ring.

"Don't tell me you already found Elizabeth." He chortled.

I stood outside Nick's building warmed by the afternoon sun and wished I had changed into my shorts and T-shirt.

"Afraid there's more. I found what looks like blood on the floor near the guest side of Nick's bed. Not a lot. Actually, not much at all."

JR didn't respond.

"I need to get it analyzed, along with fingerprints, and quick. Look, I can't say what happened here, and for all I know, it may be nothing. We can't rule out blood until we do tests."

"How did Nick react when you discovered it?" He sounded subdued.

I watched a late model Infinity drive by, then turned back to the building. "Kind of numb, but given the circumstances, I'd probably feel the same. Unless, it was one of those 'oh shit, you got me,' moments."

"Let's hope not. Okay, I know someone who should be able

to help. He retired from the force a few years back. Good guy. Lives in Miami, and he's very…resourceful." JR paused. "I hope Nick didn't open up a can of worms."

I nodded into the phone. "Let's hope not."

Upstairs, I found Nick on his computer researching the hell out of anything related to crime investigations.

"Don't make yourself crazy. JR knows a guy who can help us find the source." I feared saying "victim". "Let's not jump to conclusions. Like I told you before, it could be nothing. Besides, if a crime had been committed in your condo, it would have been messier."

Nick stopped typing.

"We just need to rule out the obvious."

"Elizabeth?"

I nodded. "I'll also have the guy dust around for fingerprints. For all we know, the blood belongs to the previous owner. We'll check that out as well."

That seemed to settle him down. He sat back in his chair and watched the ceiling fan spin around. "I never had the floors scraped."

"There you go. Did you get a chance to meet the sellers? Or was the closing done by mail?"

"I met them, nice couple. Both in their late thirties. Ryan and Nicole Lambert. It was a quick sale—motivated sellers, which saved me some money. Anyway, Ryan received a promotion from his company and needed to fly out to Chicago immediately. Nicole requested a transfer with her company and stayed behind with her parents until it came through."

I nodded. "Can you reach her, or better still, the broker?"

Nick thought a moment. "I still have the broker's business card inside my office. You want me to ask if she noticed blood on the floor?"

"*Stain.* You don't want her to clam up if you're asking about a possible abuse situation. If she didn't notice, maybe she can provide the wife's number."

"Got it." He took off inside. A few minutes later, I heard him on the phone, and when he returned, he said, "The story just changed. Nicole never requested a transfer. Turns out she and the broker are close friends. She was happy to tell me that Nicole filed for divorce and went back to her maiden name. Apparently, the happy couple wasn't that happy. And as far as joining the creep—her words—in Chicago, that never happened." Nick continued the saga, his dissatisfaction coming through at the end. "Jerk, I hope he gets what he deserves."

Either the Lamberts put on a show for Nick—no red flags—or he was a bad judge of character, which seemed ironic given his profession.

"And the broker just spilled the beans on the nice couple?"

"She helped Nicole arrange the sale, including inspection of the premises." He paused. "But she hadn't noticed anything out of the ordinary, like stains on the bedroom floor, though, off the record, she admitted there was physical abuse in their marriage. The broker mentioned something about him slamming her against the headboard, so it wouldn't have surprised her if blood stains existed somewhere."

Nick stopped. "So, if that stain is blood, it probably belongs to one of them. I'm guessing the wife." His face turned grave. "But Elizabeth is still missing."

NINE

I was debating calling JR when he called me. "You're all set, Hank. You'll be getting a call from Joe Gallagher. I told him what you needed, and he said he'd see what he could do—within legal limits, of course."

"There's been a development." I stepped out of earshot.

"*Another* development?"

I explained what we learned about the cute couple who sold their condo to Nick.

"So, they were happy in appearances only."

"Looks that way, and according to the broker, who happens to be the ex-wife's friend, the husband was rough with her. She moved out and filed for divorce. Probably the reason for the...stain."

"If that were the case, the guy would have probably cleaned the place up before the wife took the matter to the cops. I'm assuming the woman is still alive."

From the living room window, I noticed a white Mazda sport convertible passing by, loud music blaring from the speakers.

"According to the broker, she still lives in the Fort Lauderdale area."

JR said, "Okay, I'll tell Gallagher he's no longer needed."

"Hold off a second. It can't hurt if he looks around. Just to satisfy my curiosity."

"Curious, huh, Hank?"

"You know me, I don't like loose ends." I paused. "I know Nick is your cousin, but I find this whole matter odd. Not that I doubt Elizabeth took off on her own, it's just that I wanna rule out that the blood was hers. And fingerprints."

JR paused. "You're assuming she's in the system."

JR was right. Elizabeth might exist, but if she wasn't in the system, finding her would be more difficult. Besides, we didn't have her surname. I would remind Nick the bedroom was off-limits until Gallagher finished investigating.

I had an eerie feeling I wasn't alone, and when I turned, Nick stood at the doorway. He looked...possessed. His eyes were glazed over, as though looking through me, like he was in a hypnotic trance.

"Hey, you okay?"

But then, he turned and disappeared into the next room. I followed and watched as he hopped back on the computer, rapidly typing away, like he was reanimated. I stood behind him. A website appeared: Find Missing Person. He entered Elizabeth, nurse, New York, and then he described her.

I'd never heard of the site and wondered how he'd found it. Then again, Nick had been searching the internet since I arrived.

"Any luck?"

He stopped typing and shook his head in slow motion like he

was exiting a trance. "Not yet." His speech sounded slurred. "I've tried everything." His words were dragging out.

"You looked like you were in a trance. Do you get that way often?" I asked, concerned.

He shook his head. "What? No. It happens when I'm concentrating. I was concentrating."

I nodded, but I knew the difference between a trance and concentrating.

A moment later, after returning to normal, he said, "You must be hungry."

I checked my fitness tracker. *Wow, it was almost five-thirty*. With little to do until Gallagher called, I said, "Now's good. How about we go to Courtney's? I'd like to look around, get a sense of where you met Elizabeth. And check with the bartender."

Nick held off.

"Or any place for that matter."

"Courtney's is good." He pushed away from his desk and rose, as though thoroughly out of his trance.

Wanting to get a sense of the neighborhood, I asked if it was within walking distance.

"About twenty minutes, if that's okay."

Sounded good. I needed to exercise my legs. "I'm ready when you are."

He got up from the computer and gave the room a quick sweep with his eyes. "Let's roll."

Courtney's Bar and Grille was located on Las Olas Boulevard, a main east/west road, the east leading to Fort Lauderdale Beach. I'd have to remember that if I had extra time for R&R.

Weekdays in January were normally busy, but at six o'clock, we pretty much had the place to ourselves.

Inside, he looked around and shrugged. "The place looks different when the band isn't playing. Fewer people, very quiet."

He pointed to the near-empty bar. "Funny, that couple is sitting where we sat." He sighed.

My eyes closed in on the bar. "Is that the bartender who served you Saturday night?"

Nick peered over. "That's him."

I followed Nick over to the bartender, who was wiping down the bar. He looked up and smiled. "Hey, Doc."

Nick returned it then introduced him to me.

"What can I get you guys?"

Except for the couple, the bar was empty, so it was easy to ask questions. I let Nick start.

"Patrick, do you remember me being here with a woman last Saturday night?"

He nodded. "I think you were here first. It's hard to remember because the place was buzzing. I recall you were here a couple of hours." He looked at Nick, then me. "Is everything okay?"

I asked, "Did they leave together?"

Patrick looked concerned and asked again, "Is everything okay, Doc?"

I let Nick answer. "She's missing."

Patrick blinked a few times, glanced around the bar. "Did you call the cops?"

"Not yet," I said. "Do you recall if they left together?"

He looked at Nick for encouragement and Nick nodded.

"Well, I think they left separately." Back to Nick. "How do you know she's missing?"

That would have been my next question.

Nick held off a moment. "We met outside. She said she wanted to freshen up first. We went back to my place and the next morning, she was gone."

He leaned closer. "You mean she skipped out in the middle of the night? That sucks."

Nick was about to continue when I said, "Thanks, Patrick, we appreciate your help." I handed him my business card and asked him to call if he remembered anything else.

He mulled over the card and nodded. "Sure."

I'd assume Patrick would get the idea from our questions. Turning to Nick, I suggested, "Okay, then, let's get a bite to eat."

We walked over to the restaurant side and were greeted by a college-aged woman named Ashley. She brought her own friendly smile and then guided us to our table.

At Ashley's suggestion, I ordered a local craft beer, Blue Monkey, and a burger, medium-well with cheddar. They threw in fries, so that made me happy. Nick ordered the same.

Ashley's long blonde hair and blue eyes may have reminded Nick of a younger Elizabeth. He smiled wistfully.

"Do you work weekends?" I asked.

"Sometimes."

"How about last Saturday night? I hear the band was loud."

"Very loud. I was here. Lots of good tippers." She smiled. "It helps pay my tuition."

"That's good," I said. "Did you notice my friend here at the bar? He was with a woman in her thirties with strawberry-blonde hair."

She studied Nick a moment. "It was crazy busy. I can't say I did. Is it important? I mean, I can ask around. Do you have a photo?" She stopped. "Are you guys cops?"

I drew a smile. "No, but it turns out my friend had a few too many and lost her phone number. I told him he's got to rethink the way he goes about meeting women."

Ashley smiled. "I totally get it. She must be hot if you're still looking." She leaned closer. "If you take a selfie and text it to me, I'll ask around. You never know." She scribbled her number on a napkin. "You seem like nice guys."

"We are," I assured.

She kept her smile. "I'll be back with your order."

"Gee, Hank, did you have to make up a story like that? I know what you were trying to do, but…"

"Okay, maybe I should have said *tipsy*. Look, if it helps us get closer to finding Elizabeth, isn't it worthwhile?"

He pressed his lips. "I guess."

I was beginning to think this was a boondoggle and wanted to be upfront with Nick.

"If we don't get results soon, I don't want to waste your money."

TEN

At nine that night, Gallagher called and told me he'd be stopping by first thing in the morning with his equipment. And did I need anything else?

Only results.

I fell asleep on the living room sofa, watching a *Friends* rerun. Still funny. Around 1:00 a.m., I got up for my usual once-a-night pee. The place was still, dark, and unfamiliar, and as a result, I entered Nick's office by mistake. He must have fallen asleep on his daybed.

I was met with the sounds of light snoring, but then Nick began talking gibberish, followed by heavier snoring. Wide awake, I was about to leave when he cried out, "I didn't mean it. Please forgive me." At least, that was what I interpreted. One helluva nightmare. I waited, wondering if Nick would become more confessional. But after a few minutes, his breathing returned to normal.

I closed the door, took a pee, and went back to the sofa. Only I couldn't fall back to sleep. I kept thinking about Nick's nightmare, wondering if it was just that.

Gallagher showed up at 9:00 a.m. sharp, equipment in hand. He was average height, mid-fifties, with gray hair and a friendly smile. After exchanging a few pleasantries—and some cop stories—I brought him to the bedroom. Nick was sitting on the bed, hands folded, eyes glued to the stain.

Gallagher looked at me, and I shrugged. After a quick introduction, he surveyed the room, dropped his equipment on the floor and asked us to leave. Two hours later, he had completed his investigation and said he'd get back soon and left.

Gallagher called late that afternoon to tell me the stain was indeed blood, O-negative—fairly rare type, and that we would have to wait for DNA results. As far as fingerprints, Gallagher matched only Nick's. He found another in a few places, including the bathroom, but they weren't in the system.

When I told Nick, he made one of those confused expressions again. "What about Elizabeth? Surely, she touched something in the apartment. I know she used the bathroom."

I shrugged. "She's not in the system. Let's wait for the DNA results to come back, but I have to tell you, if Elizabeth isn't in the system, we're back to square one."

Apparently, Nick didn't care for my straightforward response and went into the kitchen. He returned with a glass of water and a prescription pill bottle of something. He removed a pill and eagerly tossed it in his mouth, then washed it down.

"It calms me."

I could use one of those myself, but he didn't offer one.

I needed to be alone for a while and asked to borrow his car.

Fort Lauderdale Beach was active: runners, bathers, cyclists, and anyone else wanting to escape the north in January. Nick had a few beach chairs in the trunk, but I needed to walk and think. With the beach to my right, I headed north, passing familiar chain-branded hotels.

Nick's depressed state didn't help my mood, and I was glad to get out for a while. Normally, at this time, Nick would be seeing patients, but he told me he'd cancelled all sessions, and I assumed it had to do with Elizabeth's disappearance. I left him at his computer researching god-knows-what.

I was troubled by his recent nightmare. "I didn't mean it. Please forgive me." Was he talking about the patient who killed herself? That he should have seen the red flags? Or was it someone else? Elizabeth?

That bothered me more. If he was responsible for her disappearance, why hire me?

After a half mile walk, I crossed the street and found an outdoor stool at a local bar called Sonny's. I ordered a Peroni. I was getting hooked. The bartender returned with a frosty glass and bottle.

"Another great day on the beach, huh?" I said with a smile. I needed small talk, and bartenders make the best therapists.

"Where in New York are you from?" he asked.

I smiled. "That noticeable?"

"Nah, it's just that most people I meet around here are from the New York area. Hell, I'm from the Big Apple. Left ten years ago." He stuck out his hand. "Jake."

"Hank." I shook his. "Eastpoint, Long Island. Actually, I'm in transition." I whipped out a business card. "If you're looking for a missing person, I'm your guy."

He took the card, studied it a moment. "A New York PI. I wish my ex was missing. Not that I'd hire you." He cracked a smile. "So, are you here for work or just soaking up the sun?"

I thought a moment. "Mostly the former." I poured beer into my glass and took a sip. "Today, I'm enjoying the beach."

Jake placed my card in his pants pocket. "Well, you enjoy, Hank."

I watched cars drive by, some looking for a parking spot, which was a luxury on the strip. I took another sip and looked out at the street. A red Mustang passed slowly, the driver's window open. A strawberry blonde? I blinked hard and took off for the street.

"Elizabeth?" I called out.

The car came to a complete stop, but as I approached, she stepped on the accelerator and sped around a car before I could get her plate number.

Excited, I called Nick to tell him I might have seen Elizabeth's car driving north on the strip. I got his voice message, which was typically addressed, except for an addendum, "If this is Elizabeth, please leave a detailed message. I miss you."

Jesus, the guy sounded unhinged.

I found the message bizarre, considering Nick told me they'd never exchanged phone numbers. I shook my head and left a message. "I'm at the beach. I think I might have spotted Elizabeth's car. Couldn't get the plate number, but, at least, it's something."

At the beach. What was I thinking?

I rushed back to the bar, paid the tab, and returned to Nick's car, eagerly waiting a response. But when he didn't return the call, I drove back to his house. He didn't answer my knock, so I used a spare key he'd provided.

"Nick," I called out, but the silence told me he was either napping, in a trance, or had gone out. I entered his office and found a note on his desk. "Got a lead on Elizabeth's whereabouts. Be in touch."

Well, that wasn't what I wanted to hear. I punched in his cell number again and got the same message, including, "Elizabeth leave a damn message already." Okay, maybe not that, but where the hell was he heading without a car, and what was he expecting me to do in the meantime?

I took a beer from the refrigerator and sat down in front of his computer. Fortunately, there was no password protection. When the screensaver popped up, it showed Nick fishing off a boat. Out of curiosity, I went into his photo file. Nick took lots of pictures. There were a few of him and his wife; at least, I assumed it was her.

Scrolling down the file, I discovered several of him and a buddy taken on a boat, or fishing from a pier. Interesting, one friend. I forwarded a photo to my cell.

I then checked his internet history, hoping to get an idea of his whereabouts, but none appeared helpful. As part of his search, Nick had included one on *me*. I snickered. What was Nick hoping to discover, that I walked on water? Hell, he already knew that. I didn't have a website yet, so he might have found a few newspaper articles about murders I'd worked on over the past couple of years. That would have given him pause.

Frustrated, I leaned back in the chair. If anyone knew about Nick's oddities, it would be his mother, only I didn't want to alarm her, and decided to call JR. He had less information on his cousin than I did, but at least he had a relationship with his aunt.

JR answered on the first ring. "Perfect timing, Hank; I just got off my shift. Anything new on the case?"

"Nick took off without telling me. He left a note saying he got a lead on Elizabeth's whereabouts. Why didn't he wait for me? Isn't that what he's paying me for?"

"You're upset."

"Damn right!"

"Look, like I said, Nick and I haven't seen each other in years. Did you contact my aunt?"

"I was going to, but I didn't want to worry her."

"You probably made the right decision. From what I remember, she's doted on him since he was a kid. You might have scared the shit out of her. I'll call her. She likes talking to me."

"Good, how about sweet-talking her into discussing Nick's frame of mind?" I settled down, then said, "I was on Fort Lauderdale Beach when a red Mustang passed by. Nick mentioned Elizabeth drove one Saturday night. The driver's side window was down, and it looked like it might have been her, the strawberry-blonde hair, anyway. I took a chance and called out to her, and she stopped. But as I approached, maybe fifty feet away, she took off."

"Did you get a plate number?"

"She was too quick." I waited a beat. "Quite honestly, JR, I feel like I'm chasing a ghost. I mean, even if it was Elizabeth, it doesn't look like she wants to be found."

"By Nick anyway."

"And another thing. We asked the bartender if he remembered a woman sitting with Nick that night. He did. But get this: they didn't leave together."

"What—"

"Nick claims she went to the ladies' room and he waited for her outside. Who knows if that's true? And now your cousin disappeared. I'll tell you, this whole situation is weird. I feel like I'm wasting my time and Nick's money."

"Fucking relatives. Okay, stay put until I get in touch with my aunt."

Waiting for JR, I searched Nick's apartment for the third time, finding nothing of consequence. I called Nick again and got the same message. I didn't bother leaving one this time.

There had been one place I hadn't ventured to: Nick's patients' file cabinet. It felt sacrosanct—not to say illegal, but at this point, I had no other option. Before opening the cabinet, I found a desk calendar, along with a daybook. I thumbed backwards through the calendar, hoping to get a sense of his state of mind, but each page was blank for months, as though Nick had no agenda.

Had Nick cancelled all his appointments all that time? I grabbed his daybook, which mirrored the calendar. Nothing… until I came across a notation Nick had circled in red: J.B., RIP.

Nick stopped his sessions since *that* day. What had he been doing? Holing up in his condo until he finally had the courage to venture out Saturday night? Looking for love? If so, perhaps he got more than he bargained for.

And now, he was somewhere—supposedly on foot, searching for that love on his own.

Removing the cabinet key from inside Nick's desk drawer, I still had reservations about searching Nick's patients' files, but then JR called, and I dropped the key on the desk.

"We have a problem, Hank. After soft interrogation, my aunt broke down. Nick is sick. At least, that's the way she described his behavior lately. He had a major breakdown soon after a patient killed herself and canceled all appointments before admitting himself into a local hospital. He discharged himself a little over a week ago."

I looked back to Nick's desk. *It now made sense.*

"Christ. So, this whole time, I've been searching for a non-existent Elizabeth."

"Can't say, but it's possible."

"Well, apparently, he was with someone that night. At least, at the bar." I began pacing his apartment. "I was probably seeing Elizabeth through Nick's lens at the beach today. I don't get it, JR, and I know I'm repeating myself, but why did Nick hire me?"

"It's probably part of his illness. He *thinks* she's real."

I sat down and punched the computer keys. Up popped the screensaver with Nick on a boat reeling in a fish.

"My aunt wanted to believe Nick. She realizes now it was a mistake. She'll pay you, of course."

"I'm not worried about getting paid. I feel sorry for the guy, and now, I don't even know where he went. I don't think it's safe for him to be out there alone, so I have to look for him."

"Hank, I'd come down, but I'm in the middle of a new case, a double homicide."

"I understand." My eyes focused back to the computer screensaver. "There's a photo of Nick fishing off a boat on his screensaver. I went through his photo file and noticed a bunch with him and a friend. It may be nothing, but Nick never mentioned a male friend. How about I send it over? Maybe your aunt knows the guy. He could be helpful."

"Good idea. I'll text it over to her."

"It's on its way. Talk soon."

I removed the cabinet key from the desk and, after a long sigh, opened it. Names appeared in alphabetical order, similar to John Hunter's patients' files I'd discovered in a warehouse after he was murdered, back when I was on the force on Long Island. There was nothing to suggest anything was out of place, and I flipped to Janice Brandt's file, the deceased patient. When I opened it and began reading, I realized something was terribly wrong.

ELEVEN

Nick Ross was on a mission to find his lovely Elizabeth. And now, he knew where she was. At least according to the caller, a woman who refused to identify herself.

"How did you get my number?"

"Are we going to play sixty questions? If you want to see her, be quick," she warned.

He hustled to the window, pulled back the curtains, and scanned the street. Nothing out of the ordinary. Only Mrs. Burke out walking her poodle.

Could the caller be trusted? Was she working with the guy who called Sunday morning? Maybe he should get Hank involved.

Nick decided to call him later with the good news. Right *now*, he needed to rush out and meet up with Elizabeth.

Hank had his car, so he opened the Uber app and requested a driver. The guy was fast, arriving in less than ten minutes. After a quick introduction, the driver said, "Nickel's bar in Pompano Beach, right?"

"Yes, and hurry." He slumped back, closed his eyes to quiet his nerves, and mumbled, "Please hurry."

The caller had claimed Elizabeth would be inside waiting. Through a dense brain fog, Nick thought, if she had been kidnapped and released, why wouldn't *she* call? Very odd. He hoped the caller wasn't playing him.

Arriving at the bar, Nick dashed inside. The place was a hole in the wall, with no more than ten stools, and occupied by four retired-looking guys.

He surveyed his dimly lit surroundings. Where *was* she?

He scurried to the bar and snatched at the bartender's arm. "I'm supposed to meet a woman here. Elizabeth. A strawberry blonde and beautiful." His eyes swept the room, then back to the bartender. "Was she here?"

The tall, aging-looking bartender with lots of gray hair tossed Nick a long, hard stare. "You her husband or something?"

Nick held the guy's gaze. "No, but she could be in danger."

"What's your name?"

He scowled. "My name? Why?"

The bartender folded his arms. "How do I know you aren't some guy who wants to harm this woman? If she was even here?"

"What? C'mon, I'm trying to help her."

The bartender leaned in. "So why are you afraid of identifying yourself?"

"Okay, fine. Nick Ross." His heart pounded.

"Do you have some ID, Nick Ross? A license works."

"This is bullshit! Elizabeth is in trouble."

The guy shrugged, then moved away.

"Hold on." Nick whipped out his driver's license and held it up. "Satisfied?"

The bartender eyed the license photo then Nick's face. "All I can tell you is she ordered a drink, kept looking around like she was worried about something or someone. I'm guessing a guy." His eyes glanced at a wall clock behind Nick. "She stayed around fifteen minutes, then ran off." He reached under the bar and passed a napkin across to him. "She left this for you."

Nick read the brief note. It was sketchy, and he could tell she was in a rush and nervous by her scratchy writing. *I'm afraid, Nick. I need to keep moving. I'll call you when it's safe.*

Nick glanced up at the bartender, then to the retired patrons, who seemed too busy chatting to notice his conversation.

Nick wiped his forehead. "Did you read the note?"

The bartender glared. "It wasn't addressed to me, pal, so no. I gather it's serious, given the look on your face."

"Sorry for the inference. Like I said, she could be in danger."

The bartender leaned in further. "Then maybe you oughta call the cops."

Nick pulled back, searched the bar again. Still no interested parties looking his way. He sat on a stool and hunched over. Should he wait here for her call? Or, like the bartender suggested, go to the cops?

"You look like you can use a drink."

Nick gazed up. "Drink?"

He nodded. "This is a bar. What's your preference?"

Nick checked the bottles behind the bar. "Anything."

The bartender shrugged, then came back with a glass of brown liquid with ice and placed it next to Nick's phone. "You look like a bourbon guy."

Nick sat quietly, not indulging in his drink, when his cell rang, which jolted him out of his seat.

"Hello?" he said, stepping away from the bar.

"Nick, it's Elizabeth. Sorry I had to leave. I was afraid he was on to me."

"Who?"

"I'll explain later."

"I've been so worried about you. Where did you go Sunday morning?" He continued toward the door.

"I'll explain later. Promise."

"But the caller, she told me you'd be here. Maybe we oughta call the police."

"No, no cops. He threatened to kill me if I did. And you. We'll figure it out when I see you."

Nick shook his head and stepped outside into the waning sun. "Okay, where are you?"

She whispered, "Where we met. Be quick. And Nick, I miss you."

TWELVE

Reading through Janice's file, I discovered rather disturbing news that, as a psychologist, must have been concerning. At the time, they were working through Janice's depression and anxiety issues: excessive and persistent worrying for no apparent reason. She had, on occasion, suffered from panic attacks.

Nick sensed Janice was holding back the true reason for these feelings, and she eventually admitted that her boyfriend/lover was married to her good friend. She began growing more restless about the conflicting situation, increasing her depression.

She constantly worried her friend would find out, tearing their friendship apart, causing tremendous conflict over the love she felt for him, which he claimed was mutual. Her doubts gradually grew as his excuses for not seeing her more frequently only added to her ever-increasing anxiety, now accompanied with nightmares.

The sessions got increasingly dark. Nick noted that "Janice began comparing me to her boyfriend and suggesting we looked alike. She started flirting with me, and later she tried seducing me, hoping it would lead to a romance. At that point, I was compelled to stop our sessions and refer her to another psychologist."

Her final commitment was admitting to her friend about the ongoing affair with her husband, in order to cleanse herself of her 'sin' and to 'beg for forgiveness.' "For this, I encouraged caution."

I sat down in a swivel chair and took a breather. This was heavy stuff, and not being a psychologist, I wondered what was going through Nick's mind.

Continuing, he wrote, "As far as comparing me to her boyfriend, I explained it as transference. It's a fairly common occurrence in therapy. Janice was transmitting her feelings toward me, but those feelings applied to someone else in her life, in this case, her boyfriend. When she resisted my explanation, I felt ethically obligated to end our therapeutic relationship, advising her I would suggest several psychologists to choose from."

I put down the file and stared at the blank computer monitor. It was a no-win situation. I pressed the enter key and typed Janice Brandt, Fort Lauderdale, deceased.

An obituary appeared, including a photo of the deceased, age thirty-three. It read that after a brief illness, Janice died peacefully in her sleep. At first, I thought I had the wrong person and went back to her file. But there it was; Nick had cut out the same obituary from the local newspaper.

Brief illness? Maybe the family needed to spare itself from the real culprit: suicide. Nick's notes made no mention of how she died, only that the family blamed him for her death.

The blame must have been a tremendous blow to his ego as a psychologist, feeling responsible for her death and ending their therapeutic involvement prematurely. His final note, however, was straightforward: 'Janice, who felt rejected by her boyfriend, believed I too rejected her, by terminating our relationship and recommending she start seeing another psychologist'.

The next day she was dead. Nick doubted it was *peaceful.*

THIRTEEN

Pompano Beach

Nick arranged another Uber and reached Courtney's in twenty minutes. He dashed inside and looked around. Again, no Elizabeth. He opened the ladies' restroom door and called out her name. When no one answered, he called the cell number she'd called him from, but it kept ringing.

And then his server Ashley showed up from the back and smiled. "Hey."

Nick hustled over to her. "Did you see her? The woman I described to you when I was here?"

Ashley pointed. "As a matter of fact, a woman fitting her description was standing near the door. She looked nervous, kept checking outside. I was going to show her your photo—it was in my bag in the back, but she took off."

Nick ran for the door and searched outside. "Elizabeth?"

His head drooped as he returned to Ashley.

"Are you okay?"

He shook his head in defeat then asked, "Did anyone else

come looking for her? A guy?" His voice heightened. "She could be in danger."

Ashley stepped back, probably sensing Nick's irrationality. "Just her. Were you supposed to meet her here?"

Nick mumbled and took off. He tried calling Elizabeth again, but still no answer. And no voicemail feature. Must be a burner.

Nick struggled to breathe, but he was too hyper. And now, he had no idea what to do. He was about to call Hank when his cell chirped.

"Elizabeth!"

"No, asshole, it's not Elizabeth."

"Who is this?" Nick pleaded. "And where is Elizabeth? You're the caller from Sunday morning who wanted me out of my condo alone, aren't you?"

"Pretty smart, Doc. And you did exactly as you were told." He chortled. "You did me a big favor. It would have been difficult dragging both of you out of the apartment." He laughed cruelly.

"I thought it was a prank! Why are you doing this? What do you want from me? From us?" Nick paced back and forth outside of Courtney's.

"Listen to me: Elizabeth doesn't exist. She's just your imagination. I'm calling to tell you to stop pursuing her ghost. Otherwise…"

Nick stopped pacing. "Hello?"

The bastard hung up.

Nick became consumed by dark, uncontrollable thoughts, which provoked the same downward spiral he had experienced when his patient died. The guilt of her untimely death consumed him, dragging him toward hopelessness.

He gazed out into the emptiness of the night, then reached into his pants pocket and removed a medication bottle. He quickly twisted off the cap and tossed a few pills into his mouth.

"Should take the edge off," he mumbled, while holding the bottle tightly in his hand.

He surveyed the street before heading east on Las Olas Boulevard. But after what appeared a lifetime, the meds hadn't kicked in, and, like a porn movie, images appeared: his best friend lying on top of his wife screwing and laughing.

"Stop," he pleaded into the balmy air, rubbing his eyes as though those hurtful images would disappear. But they remained vivid and he opened the bottle for more relief.

Trudging along, Nick gazed out at the lights ahead. Maybe Elizabeth was there waiting for him. He had to hurry, but his heavy feet held him back. More imagery, this time of Elizabeth crying for help.

"I'm almost there."

More flashbacks. Janice lying in a coffin. "Oh, Janice, I'm so sorry."

Nick's head continued to swirl, but he was determined to keep moving. Only a few more blocks to the light.

When he arrived, he realized the place looked oddly familiar. He had reached the famous Elbo Room beach bar. His parched mouth and the lively atmosphere drew him in for a quick drink before continuing his search for Elizabeth.

He gazed at the crowd outside the bar. Their appearance was strange, dressed as though they were at a costume party. And they were laughing. At him? He hastily brushed past them and was hit by wall-to-wall people. Straining to find the bar, he flagged down the bartender and stuttered an order for a whiskey neat.

He downed it and ordered another.

Nick's head was now swimming from all he'd ingested, but he knew he had to continue his search. He pulled back from his stool, almost losing his balance, and weaved his way through the maze of revelers. Why was he here again?

Right, Elizabeth. His eyes glazed eastward and stopped when he saw the Fort Lauderdale Beach welcome sign. Maybe Elizabeth was on the beach. He pushed himself a few more steps until his feet hit the white sand.

The waning moon made it difficult to see anything, and with great effort, Nick worked his way down to the water drawn by the relaxing ocean sounds, which provided a reprieve from the demons. But only temporary.

Nick sighed. "I failed you, Elizabeth."

Overwhelmed by the rapidly consumed intoxicants and a feeling of despair and hopelessness, Nick collapsed onto the warm white sand and into darkness.

FOURTEEN

Desperate, I decided to stop at Nick's office off Las Olas Boulevard in search of any possible direction in the case. I recalled seeing his business card on his desk, along with a half-dozen keys on a key chain and a calendar. I grabbed a card and the key chain, hoping one would fit the office door.

Downstairs, I was about to enter Nick's car when I noticed a piece of lined paper underneath the windshield wiper. It read, *Meet me at Colee Hammock Park at seven-thirty tonight if you want to see Elizabeth.* The note included a phone number. I assumed the note was directed to Nick, but I decided to meet—whomever—on my own. I'd just have to Google the place. My eyes swept the area and noticed a woman walking toward me with her poodle.

As she approached, she gave me a grave, almost accusatory look.

"That's Nick Ross's car."

I smiled. "I know, I'm a friend. You must be his neighbor." I watched the poodle take a pee on the grass.

"I am, and we watch out for each other. You don't look familiar."

I wasn't about to mess with this woman, especially since she had a killer miniature poodle with her. "He said I could borrow it. That okay?" I held up the car keys.

She scowled. "Don't be a smart-ass, sonny." She glanced over at Nick's building and sighed. "Poor thing. How is he?"

Her tone softened.

"The same, I'm afraid. How was he when you last saw him, Mrs....?"

"Burke." She pulled back on the leash. "And this is Tiger."

I waved at Tiger.

She stepped closer as though ready to reveal a national secret. "That's just it. I haven't seen him in quite a while. He must be in a funk ever since."

I wasn't interested in piecemeal information, so I said flatly, "You mean the patient."

She looked confused. "No, the wife and baby."

Baby? Stunned, I sat in the car, thinking: why hadn't Nick mentioned his wife was pregnant? What else was my client holding back?

According to Mrs. Burke, who found out from a neighbor, Nick's wife—divorce was imminent—was pregnant at the time the car crashed into a live oak tree. Both she and the baby had died.

I couldn't help but wonder if Nick was the father. By itself, the accident was tragic, but if the impending divorce had been connected to his best friend being the father, that would really suck.

I held off driving to Nick's office, and by seven that night, I arrived at Colee Hammock Park. Parking the car, I surveyed the grounds. Not knowing who would show up, I'd brought my trusty

Glock. The one-acre park on the Tarpon River was lush and beautiful, and I found a bench near the entrance.

At exactly seven-thirty, with no one around, I called the number, hoping to hear a trill or ping or chirp. Nothing. I looked around and wondered if I'd been set up.

Within minutes my cell rang out and I answered immediately.

"Hello," I said quickly.

"You're not Nick."

My eyes darted about. A woman's voice. She'd been watching me, but from where? I craned my neck around. Frustrated, I returned, "And you're not Elizabeth." Of course, I hadn't a clue.

"I need to talk to Nick—alone."

"That's not possible right now. Besides, he wants to speak only to Elizabeth." A few cyclists sped by and my eyes followed them to the exit. "So, where is she?"

"How do I know I can trust you? You could have taken the paper I slid—"

"Under Nick's windshield wiper. That's true, but I didn't. All I know is you and Elizabeth are screwing around with my friend's head. What do you want from him?"

The caller remained silent.

"Well?"

"It's personal."

"I'm sure it is. But if you want to get to Nick, you'll have to go through me."

"Fuck you."

She hung up. I watched for a woman leaving the park, but after a few minutes, my cell rang.

"Change your mind?"

"Elizabeth's in trouble, okay?"

I stood and casually walked toward the exit, waiting for her voice. "Go ahead."

A sigh. "You're right; I'm not Elizabeth. I'm her sister. She's

72

been staying with me, and not because she's looking for a new job. She's looking for a new life. Her husband is hunting her. She managed to escape once, and he isn't taking it too well. He's crazy and threatening to harm her and anyone in his way."

My eyes shifted behind me. Where was she? "Like Nick."

"Unfortunately, yes. I'm afraid he's going to kill her when he finds her. Oh, God, I can't believe her situation."

"Slow down. Nick never mentioned a husband. How do I know you're not conning me?"

"Because I'm not. Hold on, I'm going to text you a photo."

After a minute, my cell pinged.

"Did you get it?"

"Hold on." I tapped on the message icon and a photo popped up, presumably of Elizabeth. Her face showed a black eye. From the hair and other description Nick had mentioned, it could be Elizabeth.

Surveying my surroundings and without a hint of her location, I proposed, "Let's meet."

FIFTEEN

At 10:30 p.m., on a balmy night, a twenty-something couple left the popular Elbo Room dive bar on Fort Lauderdale Beach and strolled toward the ocean, hand in hand. After an evening of drinks and heavy flirtation, they decided to make the night complete by having sex on the beach (not the drink). First, they had to find a secluded spot.

Seriously? Like the beach was full of bathers at *that* hour.

A warm breeze ruffled their hair as they headed to the water's edge. After dipping their toes into the foamy saltwater, the couple embraced, followed by a long, lasting kiss. They moved on, their senses heightening, searching for just the right spot.

"What's that?" The woman with long brown hair and hazel eyes stopped in her tracks. She pointed twenty feet away.

Her blond-haired male companion turned. "Damn, it looks like a body."

The woman recoiled. "Let's get out of here!" She pulled on his arm.

"Hold on. Let's get a better look. He could just be drunk."

"He?"

"Or she." The guy tried moving on, but the woman yanked him back. "What if he's dead?"

Scratching his light beard, he said, "We might have to call the cops."

"No, no, no, no. Can't do that."

He turned. Her eyes were wide with fear. "Why not?"

"I can't be found around here if the cops come. Hell, I'm not supposed to be here with you, or anyone." Goosebumps covered her skin. "I have a fiancé—"

"Whoa, you never said anything about a fiancé." He broke free from her arm. "So, we were gonna have sex and then you'd take off?"

She shrugged, rubbing her bare arms. "What can I say? My—he doesn't like the beach. Apparently, you do."

The guy shook his head. "Go ahead, beat it. I'm gonna check on the guy." He walked over and peered down. He wasn't dead, but he was curled up on the moist sand, his body wet and shivering from the incoming tide. And he was mumbling.

The blond nudged him. "Hey, mister, are you okay?"

The guy kept mumbling. The blond, now by himself, said, "I'm gonna call for help, okay?" He peered up at the street. His companion and potential sex partner took one last look down his way, then disappeared.

So much for getting laid on the beach. He punched in 911 on his cell and waited.

When the paramedics arrived, the man was still curled up. One of the paramedics removed a driver's license from his now-soaked pants pocket.

Nick Ross.

He also found an empty prescription pill bottle of Xanax, two wet, but readable business cards, and a cell phone. One from a private investigator, and the second, a Doctor Martin Powers from Coral Springs General Hospital.

A medic wrapped him in a disposable polyester blanket, and with his partner, placed Nick on a stretcher. Shaking and disoriented, he kept mumbling something about Elizabeth.

Colee Hammock Park

Elizabeth's sister told me to meet her on the north side of the park. She'd be sitting on a bench. When I arrived, I noticed a woman, bathed in the glow of a nearby streetlight, sitting at the edge of a bench. Her feet were shaking, and her head kept shifting back and forth.

I smiled. "Just me."

She didn't return the smile.

"Hi." She looked as though she was ready to bolt.

"It's safe," I assured, my smile widening. "I'm Nick's friend."

From his description of Elizabeth, her sister could easily pass for her double. Despite her tired eyes, she was quite attractive, dressed in tight jeans and a loose floral blouse.

She looked beyond me. "Is it true that Nick's not available?"

"Afraid so. I have no idea where he is. All I know is he was supposed to meet your sister. He left a message saying he received a tip as to her whereabouts." I shrugged. "I was the one who found your note on his car windshield."

Her eyes held mine. "Whenever Elizabeth called, she was always on the run. I guess she couldn't wait for Nick. Not good." She surveyed the area, then returned her gaze to me.

"No, I suppose not," I agreed. "And, by the way, your name would help in our conversation. I'd like to know who I'm talking to." I tried getting a read on her face, but her lips tightened with tension.

She ignored the question at first, probably still wondering if I was friend or foe.

"Amanda. My name is Amanda."

"Hank. Nick hired me to find your sister after she disappeared."

"So, you're not a friend."

"Like I said, he hired me, though we've become close since I arrived." I smiled.

She dismissed my sarcasm and sighed.

"What can I say, Nick's in love." I handed Amanda my business card.

She studied it a moment. "You're a private investigator?"

I thought that was inferred. I nodded.

She slipped my card in her jeans pocket. "This has been very crazy, Mr. Reed."

"Hank, please."

"Hank. Which is why I'd like more answers."

Amanda held off a moment. "Follow me."

We entered a red Mustang and I realized, "That was you I saw on the strip today. I called out 'Elizabeth,' and you took off."

She turned to me and nodded. "I was searching for her, and when you yelled out her name, I got scared, thought you might have been Terry, and sped out of there. Sorry." With that, she depressed the door locks. Now she was freaking me out.

"Terry's a mental case. A dangerous one. I told my sister years ago not to get involved with him. But Elizabeth insisted he was a good guy and wound up with the loser. The truth is Elizabeth was always attracted to bad boys. Hence, she and Terry were a perfect match." She sighed.

"I gather Terry's the husband."

"The worst kind. He gambles, drinks, not all there in the head, and hangs out with unsavory friends. Need I go on? Anyway, after being mentally abused for years, Elizabeth finally had the courage to leave him." Amanda paused, swallowed hard. "She should have done it a long time ago, but what can I say? She was in denial."

Amanda placed her hands on the steering wheel, gripped it. "So, after he hit her—she swore only once—that photo I texted you, she took off from her home in upstate New York and headed to Florida. That was over three weeks ago." She bit her lip. "Elizabeth waited until her face healed before going out."

"That's when she met Nick."

A nod. "It was love at first sight. He must be a great guy."

I couldn't attest to Nick's character since I didn't know him very well, but my guess was he wasn't a bad boy.

A car blasting loud rap music rolled by, pausing for a moment, then drove past us, along with the noise.

She pulled the rearview mirror in her direction, searched the street.

"It's okay. They're just kids."

It took a moment for her to regroup before nodding.

I said, "Wasn't it chancy, your sister coming to you? I mean, she must have known her husband would look there first."

Amanda shifted to me. "Actually, my place was the second."

Coral Springs General Hospital

Paramedics transported Nick to Coral Springs General where an intake nurse brought him to a room. By then, he was no longer unresponsive, but still incoherent.

Doctor Powers, a short, stout man in his mid-fifties with receding gray hair, was Nick's admitting physician from a previous stay and on duty again. Nick was dead asleep when Powers arrived at his room, questioning if he had released him too soon last time, when he noticed a card on a nightstand. A PI's business card, 'Hank Reed'.

He wondered whether Nick's current condition had something to do with hiring this Hank Reed guy. Since his patient was unable to explain his current circumstances, he decided to investigate for himself. He snatched up the card, returned to his office, and dialed the PI. His message was simple and terse: "This is Doctor Martin Powers from Coral Springs General Hospital. Please call me as soon as possible."

Powers removed Nick Ross's patient file and reviewed it. He remembered his patient well: a psychologist who had experienced several significant tragedies, almost simultaneously leading to what is in laymen's terms "a nervous breakdown." Ross had realized he couldn't function and voluntarily admitted himself for observations.

Powers stopped reading the file, sat back in his comfortable black leather chair, and contemplated Nick Ross's situation. What intrigued him about this patient and his current condition? Sure, he had gone through a myriad of emotional traumas in a short period of time, but he was a psychologist and surely, had seen similar setbacks in other patients throughout his years of experience. There was something more going on with Nick and Nick was determined to find out what was going on in his world.

Colee Hammock Park

My cell phone rang, but I didn't recognize the number and let it continue to voicemail. If it was important, they'd call back.

I asked Amanda, "You said you were the second person Elizabeth contacted. Who was the first?"

Her face stiffened. After a long sigh, she said, "Her therapist back home."

"Okay," I said tentatively. "And?"

"I told you Terry was crazy. He never warmed up to the idea that Elizabeth was seeking help, especially when she returned home after her sessions happy and upbeat. He was jealous and certain she was sleeping with the guy, which she told him was ridiculous. She had more on her mind than sleeping around. She was seeing the therapist to help her get through her rocky marriage."

Amanda stopped. "Elizabeth contacted her psychologist soon after she decided to leave Terry. Knowing my sister had made a breakthrough, he supported her decision and wished her well, advising her that she could call him anytime." She paused. "Elizabeth wanted to see Doctor Shapiro one last time, to thank him personally. Big mistake."

I had no idea where Amanda was going with this. "What am I missing?"

"Doctor Shapiro is dead."

I straightened. "When?"

"The day after Elizabeth took off. Someone broke into his office that night while the doctor was there. He'd been strangled."

I sucked in a breath. "Jesus, how do you know this?"

"It was all over the media. This wasn't some random robbery gone wrong, Hank. I'm sure Terry grabbed Elizabeth's records from the files. My sister told Craig—that's what she called the doctor, damaging stuff that could implicate Terry. She blames herself, of course, for his death."

"Did she call the police?"

Her eyes answered. "She was afraid to, and I don't blame her. Like I said, Terry has friends everywhere, maybe even here in

Fort Lauderdale." She sighed. "My sister escaped from him once down here. Terry's not gonna let it happen again."

I thought of Nick's predicament and was certain he had no knowledge of Terry or what he was capable of. And now, Nick might be a liability.

"What I don't get is how Terry knew your sister was staying with Nick last Saturday night. He even had Nick's phone number and address." I shook my head. "God knows what else the bastard had."

"I swear, Hank, I have no idea, but he's capable of finding things out. Like I said, he has connections." She held off a moment. "Nick has been lucky…so far. He could wind up like Craig Shapiro."

I looked outside the front windshield. We were facing the park, which was dark except for a few streetlights. Not knowing if we were alone, I was tempted to have Amanda turn the car around and face the street but figured it would freak her out even more. So, I tweaked the rearview mirror in my direction.

So far, so good. "Where is Elizabeth now?"

"I wish I knew. She keeps moving around and calls me when she feels safe."

I nodded. "You should stay away from your house for a while. Until this Terry business is finished. It's not safe for you either, Amanda. You married?"

She hesitated. "Yes."

"Kids?"

Her eyes widened. "No, and you're scaring me."

"You'll have to tell your husband what's going on, unless—"

"He's away on a business trip."

"Till when?"

"A week or so. Do I need to call him?"

I thought a moment. "Not unless you think he might return sooner."

She shook her head. "Probably not."

I was hoping we could resolve this Terry business before that. "I'd invite you to Nick's place, but I'm afraid it's not safe there either."

"And you're staying there?"

"I am."

"Is that wise?"

My hand pressed against my ankle holster. "I have a weapon."

"So, you could protect me."

I laughed. "Thanks for the confidence. Let's not take a chance."

SIXTEEN

Coral Springs General Hospital

A t eleven that evening, Doctor Powers placed Nick Ross's file back in the cabinet, locked the drawer, and took the stairwell to the second floor. By then, Nick had been given a normal saline IV drip for dehydration.

He peered inside Nick's room and found his patient lying in bed, staring half-dazed at the ceiling.

He tapped lightly on the door, but Nick remained motionless. Powers eased himself inside and sat across from him on an upholstered chair.

"Hey, Nick, it's Doctor Powers. Martin. How are you doing?"

Nick's eyes remained unfocused.

Powers peered down at the PI's business card and asked, "Who's Hank Reed?"

Nick blinked for a second and turned his head slightly as though he had a moment of lucidity.

"Says he's a private investigator. One of the paramedics

found it in your pocket. Is he a friend, or did you hire him for something?"

Still no response. Powers waited a few moments longer before getting up to leave. When he reached the door, he heard Nick mumble what sounded like, "Need to find Elizabeth."

Colee Hammock Park

Amanda made a call, presumably to Elizabeth. They spoke for a moment before she said, "You have Billy's car? Okay, stay there. We'll meet you at—hold on." She checked the car clock. "Around eleven. I'm thirty minutes away and have Nick's PI with me. Be safe."

I smiled. "So, you know where she is?"

Amanda hesitated.

"What, you don't trust me by now?"

She held up a hand. "Sorry, I'm just a little uptight. Where's your car?"

I looked past her and pointed. "It's Nick's."

"Okay, follow me."

"C'mon, Amanda. What if I lose you? Look, you guys need me more than I need you. If you're going to play games, I'm out of here. Open the door."

"Wait!" She grabbed my arm. "Leave your car. We're going to the airport."

Doctor Power's Office

Doctor Powers returned to Nick's file, looking for any notation mentioning this Elizabeth woman. Finding her was what he believed his patient had mumbled. Was he to assume that Nick's breakdown had something to do with her? The EMS folks found nothing on him that mentioned Elizabeth. He wondered if foul play was involved, but there was no hint of a dispute: blood, bruises, ripped clothing.

Powers glanced up at the wall clock. He lifted Hank Reed's business card from the file. Why hadn't he called back? Powers was desperate and punched in the PI's number one more time.

SEVENTEEN

Fort Lauderdale Strip

By ten-fifteen that evening, Terry Bash was majorly pissed. He hated Fort Lauderdale, not that he'd been there before. He loathed the slow traffic and the schmucks who refused to use turn signals.

The beach road sucked more. Pedestrians strolling across the street like they owned it. He should run down a few. They'd learn. But bitching didn't help. He needed to find Elizabeth *again*, and quick.

When he first arrived in Fort Lauderdale, he went directly to Amanda's house. He knew her all too well from New York when he tried putting moves on her. Unfortunately, she resisted, took off for Florida, and never returned.

Terry chortled. Didn't matter, he had Elizabeth. When he'd arrived at Amanda's place, she was alone and scared shitless. Terry couldn't blame her, especially after he and his sidekick had tramped through the house. He threatened, "If I come back and find her here, you won't like it."

Then last Saturday night, Terry got lucky. One of his under-lings, a guy named Blade—he loved Spyderco military knives—had stopped off for a drink at a place called Courtney's in Fort Lauderdale and saw Terry's wife sweet-talking with some guy.

What luck!

Blade had followed her and watched as she parked in front of a residential building not far from Courtney's. She waited until the guy from the bar showed up and parked not far from hers. All smiles. They went inside.

Blade planted a tracker under the car she was driving, and then took down the guy's plate number. He made a few calls and bingo: Terry's wife was doing some guy named Nick Ross. Doctor Nick Ross. What was up with her and doctors?

Rather than barge in on the couple, Terry had pulled a stunt and with one call, scared the hell out of the guy! When the doc left his place—no cojones—Terry and Blade appeared. Eliza-beth's eyes bulged when she saw them. She must have thought the scaredy-cat doctor was returning, only she thought wrong. He swept her out of the place then had Blade fix up the condo, including replacing sheets, as though she'd never been there.

Terry snickered to himself.

And the call to the deli, how cool was that? He bet this Ross fellow peed himself when he returned home. Would he call the cops? If so, Terry would deal with it.

He sneered through the windshield in his black Ford F-150 and pounded the steering wheel with his fist. He'd had the bitch, but she slipped out of the motel bathroom window a few hours after he snatched her.

Stupid! He'd believed her when she swore she'd return home with him. Had to fix herself up in the bathroom first.

Right! Last time he'd fall for that shit.

Terry settled down, took a breath. *I got your number, Doctor Nick Ross.* Oh, yeah. One thing was certain: no more bad decisions.

And then his cell went off.

Blade. He listened intently and when his underling finished, he smiled. "Nice work, Blade Man. Remind me to give you a raise." Terry snickered and hung up. He turned to his sidekick, Sammy. "We got her."

A wide smile. "Where to?"

"Gotta make a U-turn and head east on Sunrise Boulevard, then shoot up to the Interstate. Christ, I can't believe I'm beginning to get familiar with this place."

Interstate I-95 Fort Lauderdale

Airport?

Amanda drove south on I-95, and when she passed Broward Boulevard, I noticed a sign for Fort Lauderdale International Airport. She exited Marina Mile Boulevard instead.

"I think you got off the wrong exit." I pointed ahead. "You did say airport, right?"

"Trust me."

I shrugged. I held my cell phone in both hands when it went off. Same unknown number as before.

Amanda eyed me. "You going to take that?"

"I'm thinking about it."

She shook her head.

"Hello," I said, annoyed.

"Hank Reed?" Friendly enough voice.

"Depends who's calling. I'm not familiar with this number. Are you a telemarketer?"

He chortled. "Afraid not. I'm a doctor at Coral Springs General Hospital. I found your card in one of my patient's belongings."

"Nick Ross?" I said, my voice rushing. "Is he okay?"

Amanda turned her head quickly, her face grave. "What's going on?"

I put up a finger. "What happened, Doctor…?"

"Powers. Martin Powers. There's a limit to what I can discuss with you given you're not family, but yes, he's fine, well, let's say comfortable. They found him at the beach."

"Beach? What the hell was he doing there?"

"We don't know because he's not in a talkative mood. Did he hire you to find someone?"

I held off a moment. "Let me call you back."

"But—"

Amanda wove a path south then east, and I wondered if she was lost. "Give me a minute." I Googled Coral Springs General Hospital, found the number, and called.

"Doctor Martin Powers." After several options, I got a live person.

"Hold, please."

When Powers got on, I said, "Okay, now we can talk."

"Oh, a PI thing. I get it."

"Good, now let's hear more about Nick Ross."

"I heard him mumbling the name Elizabeth as though she was lost or missing. Does that name mean anything to you?"

When I hesitated, Doctor Powers continued, "I'm thinking maybe he hired you to find her. Just a guess, of course."

"He did. I'm hoping to connect with her tonight. Is it your professional opinion that Nick's condition has to do with losing her?"

Doctor Powers hesitated. "I'm sorry, but I can't reveal very much. I'm hoping you understand and are open to a one-way conversation, at least for the time being. Your responses could help my patient, Mr. Reed."

"Call me Hank. To answer your question, at first, I didn't

know if Elizabeth even existed. I now know she does. There are complications of which I can't reveal at this time. I hope you understand."

"Touché, Hank."

I turned to Amanda and nodded. "I'm with her sister. We're on our way to meet her."

"I'm relieved to hear that. Nick has family nearby, so if his mother agrees, we can talk at length later."

"That works for me."

"And if you see Elizabeth, please impress upon her the importance of a visit. I believe it would help Nick."

"I plan on it, Doc."

EIGHTEEN

Inside West Perimeter Road

Terry's beet-red face reflected his anger. He jammed on the brakes then pounded the steering wheel. The headlights tunneled a glow into the narrow dirt path.

"Shit, I can't go any farther. Elizabeth could be anywhere. She's probably calling the cops as we speak."

"You know she won't call them," Sammy assured. "She's got too much at stake."

He backed out of the wooded area. "You're probably right, only I don't wanna take chances. Let's get out of here."

"You think someone tipped her off? She ran off as soon as we entered the parking lot."

Terry remained quiet, but his grip on the steering wheel suggested he'd been defeated again. He mumbled, "Bitch."

When they reached the main road leading to the interstate, he said, "She probably saw us coming. Hell, if Blade hadn't placed a tracking device on her cell phone when we first nabbed her, we wouldn't have known she'd be here. Next time, Elizabeth. There will be a next time."

"You said Blade intercepted a call between Elizabeth and some woman."

"Probably her sister." Terry narrowed his eyes. "I shoulda been more threatening when I raided her house. I'm not finished with those two."

Terry drove back to the Rustic Motel in Davie, the place Elizabeth had escaped from. He turned off the engine and gazed up at his new room on the third floor. Let her try jumping out of that bathroom window.

West Perimeter Road Fort Lauderdale International Airport

Amanda turned onto West Perimeter Road. "What was that all about?"

I kept my eyes on the road, wondering where we were headed. "Nick's in the hospital. Sounds like he might have had a nervous breakdown."

"Breakdown?" She jerked the steering wheel crossing over the dividing line, then pulled back and steadied herself.

"What happened? Does it have to do with my sister? This is crazy."

"Take it easy." I touched her hand. "It's too early to ask the whos or whys, and the doctor isn't saying much since I'm not a relative. He needs Nick's mother's permission, which shouldn't be a problem." I paused. "I doubt it had anything to do with your sister." The less Amanda knew, the better.

"You sure?"

Of course, I'm not sure. But if there was any hope for a Nick—

Elizabeth relationship, I sure as heck wasn't about to mention Nick's oddities, like trances and that stuff.

"Pretty sure. The doctor thinks a visit from her might help. He said Nick mentioned your sister's name." I hoped Amanda wouldn't continue asking questions, and she didn't. For now. As we passed the Naval Air Station Museum, I noticed a plane approaching the airport and realized we were meeting Elizabeth somewhere outside the airport perimeter.

"Ever hear of the Ron Gardner Aircraft Observation Area? Been here for years."

"Ron or the observation area?"

Amanda laughed lightly. "He was an Aviation Department employee and airport friend. It was dedicated to him."

"Let's hope Ron brings us good luck."

"We're almost there."

Suddenly, from around the bend, an oncoming vehicle's headlights almost blinded us, causing Amanda to pull the wheel hard to the right.

"Crazy bastard! He had to be going sixty."

I glanced back. It looked like a dark pickup truck. As we approached the parking lot, I noticed a handful of cars parked, all facing the runway. Great views.

Amanda's eyes swept the area, but the waning moon wasn't helpful. All the car colors blended in like one big dark mass. "She should be here." Amanda tucked her car in the back for a better view of movement, but there wasn't any. She pulled out her phone and speed-dialed a number.

"We're here, Elizabeth. Where are you?"

She turned to me. "It went straight to voicemail." Amanda was about to jump out of the car when I grabbed her. "Hold on. What was she driving?"

I could see Amanda was straining to find the car.

"Amanda, make and model!"

"Sorry. A black Honda Civic. It belongs to my husband."

The lights from the runway and planes queuing up parallel to us weren't at the best angle to get a good view of the parking lot. I counted six cars. All but one had their lights off.

Odd.

"Stay here." I got out and started for the one with its lights on, Amanda trailing. So much for taking orders. Twenty feet away, I realized it was a black Honda Civic.

I turned. "Call her."

As I continued to the car, jet engines revved up behind me, and I struggled to hear a cellphone chirping. I dashed for the car and opened the driver's side door. A phone on the seat, no driver, engine off.

Amanda caught up. "That's Billy's car."

"Your husband?"

"Yes. Oh, God, Terry must have taken her. He'll kill her, I know it!"

How did Terry know she'd be here?

I held her by the shoulders, but she kept wailing. "He'll kill her, I know it."

Thankfully, no one appeared to be interested in us. I activated my phone flashlight, shined it in different directions, then stopped. "You said Terry showed up at your house. What was he driving?"

"Some kind of pickup truck. Why?"

I kept my hunch to myself, but it had to be Terry's truck that had passed us. And at his speed, he'd be long gone by now.

My light shone on a wooded area behind where Elizabeth had parked. I looked back toward the runway. There was no way she could have climbed over the fence, given the barbed wire at the top.

"Check with those cars' occupants, see if they saw anything unusual."

"Where are you going?"

I was already rushing to the woods. "Elizabeth," I shouted. "It's Hank and Amanda. If you're in there, it's safe to come out."

I walked another twenty feet and called out again. Except for the wind slapping against the trees, it was quiet.

Minutes later, Amanda called out to me. I ran back to the opening. She had her phone light on and directed me to her. When I caught up, she was conversing with a woman inside a Smart car. Her window was lowered, and I could see she was alone except for an alcohol flask companion. When she noticed my stare, she attempted to hide it deep in the seat.

"Relax, I'm not a cop."

"Tell him what you told me."

The woman averted her eyes. "Like I told her, I must have fallen asleep. At some point, a car horn woke me up, and I think I saw someone running into the woods. Look, it could have been nothing."

"What about a truck dashing out of the parking lot?"

"Think so. Like I said, I'd been nodding off and on."

Right.

"Better ease up on that." I nodded at the flask.

She started the engine, powered up the window, and gave me the bird.

"It had to be Elizabeth running away."

"I already checked. If she was in there, she would have heard me calling her." I paused. "I think Terry was driving that truck and almost ran us off the road. He might have her."

The roar of an airplane engine drowned out what Amanda was saying, but I got the gist: "The crazy bastard is violent."

I wasn't a fan of jet fuel, and with the evening breeze, it permeated the air and made me nauseous. "Look, there's not much we can do here."

Back in the car, I told Amanda we had to get the police involved. Especially if Terry snatched Elizabeth.

"No cops!" Her eyes met mine. "No cops."

There wasn't fear in her eyes, just resolve.

"What are you not telling me?"

She gazed out the window. "Terry knows people."

We all know people. "Okay?"

Amanda squirmed.

"Look, if Terry has your sister, what difference does it make how many people he knows? He could have killed her when he had the chance." I paused. "Or maybe not. What's going on, Amanda? There's something you're leaving out."

Amanda dangled a set of car keys.

"You take your husband's car. He knows yours. If he's waiting out there, he'll go after me." Of course, if Terry had Elizabeth, he wasn't interested in Amanda.

NINETEEN

Inside West Perimeter Road

Elizabeth ran deeper into the woods. No one could drive through these trees unless they had a tank, and Terry wasn't driving one.

She stopped running when she felt safe, then leaned against a Ficus tree and vomited. That was close. She knew what her crazy husband was capable of—especially now that she'd escaped once by lying to him about returning to their home.

But now, she'd tested his patience. Terry had already killed her New York therapist because he thought she was having an affair with the guy. He was on the warpath, and she feared he would stop at nothing to get her back, even if it meant killing another therapist: Nick Ross.

While surrounded by nothing but darkness and the occasional smell of raccoon—which she was petrified of—Elizabeth thought of Nick Ross. She was totally smitten. He was caring and loving and wasn't looking for a one-night stand. She had to keep him safe. Them safe. But how?

Elizabeth wiped her soiled mouth, spit out residue from a slice of pizza she'd grabbed on the run, and carefully made her way back to the parking lot. When she reached the clearing, she stopped and looked around.

She noticed two cars heading out. Amanda's cars. She tried running after them, but it was too late. Amanda and Hank Reed—she assumed—must have thought Terry had taken her. She wanted to scream.

Elizabeth leaned her tired body against a Queen Palm. Thank God she'd taken her handbag. She removed her other cell phone—a burner—and was about to call her sister to turn around and pick her up, then stopped.

What if Terry was still lurking around, maybe waiting for her somewhere on West Perimeter Road? He knew the car she was driving. Terry wasn't an idiot; he'd know she'd have to return to the car eventually, and he'd be watching just outside the safe perimeter zone.

Oh, God! What if he cuts off her car? Or Hank's? Would he harm them?

Elizabeth inhaled jet fuel and became nauseous. She held back, heaving again. She knew she needed to get out of there. Fast.

Elizabeth remembered passing a building near the parking lot. Naval Museum or something. She skirted the back of the parking lot and dashed across the dark, lonely road and climbed a few steps to the entrance. It was closed, which suited her fine.

She really only had one option: Uber. She removed the burner from her bag and made contact.

Elizabeth Bash had managed to outmaneuver her crazy husband once again. But she wondered for how long.

While following Amanda to the interstate, I wondered why the sisters refused to go to the police. Body language spoke a lot about a person during difficult times, but I couldn't get a read on Amanda.

I called her. "Time is of the essence. If you want me to help you and your sister, tell me now: what is Elizabeth up to?"

Amanda sighed into the phone. "Fair enough. Elizabeth was bored with her job, and not having kids, decided to go into business. Maybe a carwash like Skyler in *Breaking Bad*. When she mentioned her idea to Terry, he thought it was great. He'd put up the funds. Turns out, he was familiar with the series, too. Only his plan was to wash other people's money, not cars. When Elizabeth found out what he was up to—only recently she swears— she demanded he stop, or else." Amanda paused. "Terry doesn't take threats lightly."

"Did she say how long the laundry business had been operating?"

"Terry was evasive and told her not to interfere in *his* business."

Continuing on the interstate northbound, I asked, "And it took her all this time to figure out what he was up to? Seriously? You told me *she* was the brains of the family."

Amanda must have taken offense to my response and nudged a little closer to the median. "She claimed she didn't know until recently, period."

I continued watching her car. "No offense. But you must admit—"

"What can I tell you, Hank? I believe my sister."

Apparently, Amanda was very protective of Elizabeth. My instinct told me Elizabeth knew what Terry was up to long before she admitted it to Amanda. Maybe she had a personal stake in that part of the business. Hence, no cops.

I could hear tears in the background, and the car again,

tittering off the lane. "Elizabeth left her phone in the car, so there's no way I can reach her. Oh, Hank, this is so bad."

"We'll find her," I assured. "Did she mention the motel she escaped from?"

"The Rustic Motel, off Federal Highway in Davie."

"Where's that?"

"Just north of the Seminole Hard Rock Hotel & Casino, on State Road 7."

"It's foreign to me, Amanda. I'll follow you. Just don't enter the parking lot. Terry might already be there. And one other thing: we haven't finished our conversation on the carwash business."

"I have a call coming in," she said quickly, and hung up.

The Uber driver pulled up to the Coastal Inn, an old, brick and mortar building with a big, obnoxious yellow and white neon sign blinking its name and "Coffee Shop".

Elizabeth ran to her unit and double-locked the door, then stripped down before jumping into the shower.

After patting herself dry, she retrieved the burner from her handbag and called her sister.

"I'm safe. Terry missed me by minutes. I took an Uber back to my motel." She perched on the bed and surveyed the room with its flower wallpaper and yellow everywhere: drapes, bedspread, and wall-to-wall shag carpeting. God, she felt dirty.

"Terry must have found out where I was heading. How the hell…?"

"Thank God you're safe. Stay put."

"I need to get out of Fort Lauderdale, Amanda." She looked in the room mirror. Her face showed fatigue—dark circles and new wrinkles.

"Nick has been looking everywhere for you! You know he's crazy about you." She stopped.

"I hear a *but* in your voice."

"Nick's been hospitalized. He's...had a breakdown. We need to find a way for you to see him—tell him you're okay." She paused. "Could be why he got sick."

"Oh, God. It's all my fault." She shook her head. "I need to see him. Can we do it?"

"You're on a burner, right?"

"Yes."

"Okay, stay put and don't open the door for anyone. I mean it, Elizabeth, no one. Hank is behind me in my car. I'll have him follow me to your motel. See you in less than a half-hour."

"Please hurry."

I glanced in the rearview mirror. The same vehicle had been following me for the past few minutes. I entered the center lane. The truck pulled out and kept a tail. I feared following Amanda, especially if she was heading toward Terry's motel. I called, but had to leave a voice message.

"I think I'm being followed. Forget Terry's motel. Keep driving and I'll call when it's safe."

As Amanda continued north, I exited at Broward Boulevard. My tail followed. So much for speculation. One good sign: if Terry had Elizabeth, he wouldn't be following me.

I made a quick right onto South Andrews Avenue then another at Himmarshee Street, finding myself in the heart of downtown Fort Lauderdale. At midnight, the streets were near-deserted. My cell chimed, and I picked it up.

"Where'd you go?" Amanda asked.

"Didn't you get my message? I think Terry's following me.

I'm sure he was waiting outside the perimeter road for Elizabeth to show up. Which means he doesn't have her."

"I know. She called me when you were calling in. Sorry. I changed plans and am driving to her motel, the Coastal Inn. What are you going to do?"

"Not sure yet."

"Be careful. He's—"

"I know, dangerous. Later." I disconnected and pulled up alongside an IMAX movie theater. The truck stopped a few spots behind me. I pressed my Glock, took a breath, and emerged from the car.

The truck remained still, so I waved and approached the passenger side, my slack arms at my sides. This wasn't what I'd signed up for, but here I was going after bad guys again. I must be crazy, but if Terry thought I knew where Elizabeth was, he'd hold off shooting.

That was my hope, anyway.

I stood next to the front passenger window and motioned the guy to roll it down. When he did, I peered inside. "Say fellas, I need directions. I'm from out of town."

Two white guys, late thirties. The passenger was skinny with a sneer, his long brown hair unkempt. He wore a black Metallica T-shirt and a gold studded earring.

The driver had a military-style haircut, dark brown, menacing eyes and a chunky build. His choice in T-shirt was Iron Maiden. A mean-looking dragon tattoo decorated his arm with a phrase at the bottom that read, "Trust No One."

I figured he was Terry.

The skinny one, trying to sound threatening, said, "Yeah, well, we're not from around here either."

"What a coincidence? So, you're lost too?"

A glare. "None of your fucking business."

The Iron Maiden guy stared and looked mean, like his tattoo.

"Okay then, you guys enjoy the rest of the evening."

The window rolled up and the driver pulled out. As he drove slowly past Amanda's car, he appeared to be looking inside.

"She's not there, asshole," I called out, then memorized the plate number.

When the truck disappeared, I called Elizabeth or Amanda, whoever picked up. "Describe Terry."

Amanda conveyed a detailed description.

"I just said hello. Not too friendly. Or his skinny sidekick, who did all the talking."

"Sammy. Another nut job."

"At least I know who they are. They'll probably follow me back to Nick's place, maybe even stay the night in the truck, which is fine with me. You guys stay put, and I'll call in the morning."

TWENTY

I was beat. It had been a trying day. Hopefully, tomorrow, I'd get a better sense of who Terry really was, but that would require my detective buddy's help.

I speed-dialed JR. He wanted an update on Nick, and I needed his help. I could hear a singer in the background—off-key—and knew my buddy detective was in a bar.

"I was just thinking of you, Hank. I'm hanging out at the Dive Bar. You remember; I took you there one night a while ago."

"How could I forget? I borrowed your knife that night."

He chortled. "Let me go outside. It's Crazy Karaoke night, and the guy singing Sinatra is killing it, and not in a good way."

I laughed. "You oughta get up there and replace him."

"Not me, amigo. The crowd would toss me out on my ass."

I could tell JR reached the street as the music died down.

"Worse than the guy singing Sinatra?"

"Hank, I don't even sing in the shower. Anyway, I was going to call you. How's Nick doing?"

I pulled into a tight spot in front of Nick's building and

peered out the window before getting out. Was I getting paranoid?

"Not well. I have to tell you, there's more going on than just a missing person, who, by the way, is no longer missing."

I laid out the details, including my encounter with Terry and his sidekick. "I need you to pull up a New York plate number. A background check on the owner, which I believe is a guy named Terry; sorry, no last name yet. See if he has a rap sheet. I'm told he washes cars for a living. Think *Breaking Bad*, if you get my drift. He's the prior missing person's husband." I paused. "For all I know, she could be in business with him, though her sister vehemently denies it. Too vehemently if you ask me. Just a feeling."

"Hank, I'm sorry I got you mixed up in this. Look, I can get a few locals involved if you need them."

"I'm good."

"Christ, my poor cousin. I hope this woman is worth it."

"Me too." I checked the street for the umpteenth time since connecting to JR. "I better get upstairs."

"What about the plate number?"

"Oh, right. It's been a hell of a day." I passed on the information, then emerged from the car and kept in touch with my surroundings. All quiet.

I took the stairs to Nick's unit. "I don't believe the guy's broken any laws in Florida, at least, not yet."

JR said, "Sounds like we need him to attempt one. I'm sure we can come up with something."

"We?"

"Hank, I'm up here, but we're in this together now."

TWENTY-ONE

I was fishing out Nick's house keys from my pocket when I noticed his door ajar. I went for my Glock and stepped closer. The door hadn't been tampered with, which meant someone had a key.

I nudged it open and listened for intruders.

Silence.

I extended my weapon hand and slowly entered. The unit was dark. Knowing Nick was in the hospital, who else would be interested in his place?

Terry.

I hit my cell-phone light and brightened up the living room, then flipped on the light switch. Nothing appeared out of place. Moving from room to room, I flipped on every switch in the condo before turning off my cell light.

I scratched my two-day growth and wondered if I'd forgotten to lock the door before leaving.

Doubt it.

Terry, not knowing Nick's whereabouts, must have decided to

screw with his head—not that he needed any help. One quick look out the window: it was deserted.

Goosebumps.

Inside the kitchen, I took a bottle of Peroni from the fridge and was about to head for the sofa when I spotted a greeting card perched on the kitchen table. I grabbed a paper towel and opened the envelope.

Dear Doc,

Sorry for your loss. Not yet, but you get the idea. Stay away. And if you run to the cops, well, think about Elizabeth.

A sympathy card with a threatening message.

I took a much-needed slug of beer, wiped my mouth with my wrist, and set the card back on the table. I doubted Terry's fingerprints were on the card or anywhere else in the condo. The bastard was careful but direct. Don't go looking for my wife or else.

I recalled JR's suggestion. We need Terry to attempt to commit a crime. Too late, he already did. Breaking and entering. Check the box.

One thing was certain, Nick's lock would be changed ASAP. *Then* I thought, *maybe not.*

Terry angled his truck down the block, clear enough to see Ross's apartment. He saw the guy he'd encountered at the IMAX theater exit and search his surroundings. Terry gave Sammy a nudge with his elbow, then chuckled.

"A little hide and seek," he said. "Catch me if you can."

As the guy entered Ross's building, Terry mumbled, "Who the hell is that jerk? And where's Doc Ross?"

"We gonna find out?"

Terry shook his head. "Nah, I'm more curious to see if he

flees the place after reading the sympathy card." He slapped Sammy on the knee and chortled. "Shit, I expect him to run for the hills."

"Yeah, but Terry, Ross isn't reading the card; the other guy is."

Terry scratched his head. "Well, shit, the doc'll read it at some point. I mean, this asshole will show it to him, right?"

He turned to Sammy, who shrugged. "Hell, if I know. We don't even know who the guy is. Maybe we shoulda asked him a few questions when we had the chance."

"Yeah, maybe."

"Could be the creep was on the phone with Ross, giving him the bad news. He'll probably pee himself."

Sammy said, "Or called the cops. Especially now that he knows we have a spare key."

Terry sneered, fingered the extra key he'd swiped from Ross's apartment the day he snatched Elizabeth—for safe keeping. "I doubt he'll go to the cops. I left a pretty direct message. Besides, he knows I can find him anytime. I just wanna make sure the fucker isn't still looking for my wife, or he's a dead man." He held off a moment, looked down the street. "I think he got the message."

"So, what do we do now? Continue looking for Elizabeth?"

Terry shook his head. He knew they'd never find her at this hour, and Blade hadn't got back on any new leads. Elizabeth was safe for now. Tomorrow was another day.

Police sirens echoed in the background, and for a brief moment, Terry stiffened. Maybe entering the doc's condo hadn't been such a good idea.

"Let's get out of here."

At eight the following morning, I waited for an Uber driver outside Nick's building. Another car-switch day. This time, I had to pick up Nick's at Colee Hammock Park, where I'd left it after meeting with Amanda. The cool, gentle air was refreshing, and I imagined sticking around after my gig was over.

I turned my head and noticed Mrs. Burke and Tiger heading my way. I waved and she waved back, holding a fresh plastic bag of poop. At least, I assumed it was fresh.

The driver pulled up before she had a chance to ask any questions. I had already spoken to Amanda and told her I'd pick up the sisters around nine-thirty. Amanda's voice was tense, and she said she hadn't slept a wink. Made sense, not knowing if crazy Terry would barge in on them.

After picking up the car, I headed to the Coastal Inn and parked before calling Amanda. I stepped out and waited a few moments. Amanda appeared first, nervous, eyes darting in all directions, then hustled over to me. Elizabeth was next. As they approached, I thought my eyes deceived me.

"What—"

"We're twins, Hank. I thought you knew that."

My eyes shot back and forth, hoping to distinguish one from the other, but the closer they approached, I knew I was in trouble.

"Identical?"

"I'm Amanda from yesterday." She smiled nervously.

Elizabeth appeared equally nervous. "Hello, Hank." She gazed over at me, smiled wearily.

"Hi," I said quickly.

"How's Nick?"

Definitely Elizabeth. I had no idea how Nick was doing, but said, "I know he'll be happy to see you."

Elizabeth pressed her lips. "I hope he'll still be interested, considering all that's happened."

I'm sure he will.

I smiled. "I don't doubt it." I turned back to Amanda, who had accumulated dark circles under her eyes overnight. "You need coffee?"

"Please." She touched my hand. "And thanks for doing this. Just being here."

"That's what I was hired to do. To find Elizabeth."

"You know what I mean." She hung onto my hand a little longer, her eyes pleading for this craziness to end.

I nodded. "Let's get some coffee."

We drove in silence. Occasionally, I'd glance in the rearview mirror. Elizabeth stared out the window, wringing her hands, and I could only imagine where her thoughts lay.

Amanda knew the hospital's location and told me a Holy Donuts joint was a block away.

She pointed, and I pulled up to the drive-thru and ordered coffees and donuts.

"The hospital is on the next block," Amanda said. "Plenty of parking around back."

After grabbing our breakfast, I drove to the hospital and parked a few aisles from the entrance. I took a sip of coffee and bit into a sugar stick.

I heard a sigh in the back seat and looked at the rearview mirror. "Ready?"

Elizabeth nodded. She hadn't touched her Boston cream, which I would make sure wouldn't go to waste.

I had called Doctor Powers, and he was pleased Elizabeth would join us. But he also told me to be prepared. Nick was still pretty much out of it.

I took one last gulp, polished off the donut, and said, "Let's go."

I turned to Amanda. "I'd ask you to join us, but I think Nick would get confused seeing both of you together."

She smiled. "Understood. I'll be here."

I got out of the car, looked around, then stuck my head in. "Call me if you need to." I left out the danger word, but I knew she understood and nodded.

Once inside, I checked the hospital directory. Doctor Powers had his own office on the third floor. After a quick knock, Powers opened the door and smiled.

"Hank?"

I nodded and introduced him to Elizabeth.

"So happy you're here, Elizabeth. I know Nick will be happy to see you."

I wondered whether Nick was capable of seeing anyone, but I kept that to myself.

"Come in."

We followed Powers inside to a standard-size room with a walnut desk, a black leather chair, and a bookcase filled with medical volumes. Framed family pictures clustered on the wall. He pointed to two leather chairs near a large window.

"Please."

Powers had a look of stoic resignation, which didn't put me at ease. I figured we were in store for a difficult visit, especially for Elizabeth. He looked at me. "Like I mentioned on the phone, Nick's mother gave me permission to discuss his condition and to answer your questions. Unfortunately, I'm afraid there doesn't seem to be much improvement since he was admitted. I'm hoping that will change once he sees you, Elizabeth." His glance shifted to her.

She smiled sadly. "I hope…"

Powers rubbed his hands and stood. "I'll take you to Nick."

TWENTY-TWO

Amanda needed a second cup of java. She also had to stretch her legs and exited the car. She waited at the light until a dozen cars flew by, then ran across the street and entered the donut shop.

After getting her coffee, she found a small table in the corner and took a much-needed sip. She thought about the dangerous situation she was in—they were in, knowing Terry would stop at nothing to haul Elizabeth back to New York.

As Amanda took another sip and gazed out the window, her mind started playing games, returning to those dark days, years ago in New York. It was why she'd left for a new life. Now, after all these years, those visions reappeared, and it frightened her. Actually, it made her angry, very angry. *Damn you, Elizabeth!*

Amanda's contempt for Billy, her soon-to-be ex-husband, was just as strong. She hated him for what he did to their marriage, and the more she thought about him, the more she got worked up.

She blinked hard to expel the demons and swore to herself.

Settle down, Amanda. She thought of Hank Reed. He seemed like a genuinely nice guy and she wondered if he was married.

Stop fantasizing.

Amanda took a long breath. As her eyes returned from the window, she sat staring at the man with the nasty dragon tattoo. She turned quickly toward the door, but it was too late to bolt.

"Hey there, sister-in-law."

She tried to leap out of her seat, but Terry grabbed her wrist, pushing her down. He smelled of sweat and whiskey.

She glared. "What do you want? And how did you find me?"

"Is that any way to treat family? Sit for a while. I'm not going to hurt you." He looked around. "Especially not here." A sinister chuckle.

"Answer my question. How did you find me? And when was the last time you took a shower?" She scowled.

Terry glared back. "I know where the doc lives. Let's leave it at that."

Amanda stiffened. That meant Terry had followed Hank this morning to their motel. She swallowed hard.

Amanda pulled free from his sweaty hands and put on her best angry face. But looking at the scary dragon on his arm, she knew what he was capable of.

"Then what do you want? I already told you everything."

Terry had his own cup of coffee. He took a long gulp, then grimaced. "Damn, this shit is boiling."

She cracked a smile, then regretted it.

He wagged a finger at her. "You haven't told me everything. Who's that guy in the doc's apartment? The smart-ass with the big mouth?"

She shrugged. "What guy?"

He looked at his cup. "This coffee is scalding, Amanda. I could toss it in your pretty face. Look, I'm getting tired of this shit and Fort Lauderdale. I got a business to run, and your sister's carwash business is suffering because she ain't there." He leaned forward, inches from her face, assaulting her nostrils. "Don't fuck with me. I know she's at the hospital with the guy. What the hell are they doing there?"

Amanda wanted to tell jerk face that the car washing business in January in upstate New York is never busy. But she knew he was referring to the 'wash.' She also knew he would gladly toss the contents of his coffee cup in her face, laugh, and casually walk away.

"So?" He shifted his cup to his other hand.

"He's a private investigator, okay?"

Terry pulled back. "Say again."

She hesitated, formed her words carefully. "Nick Ross hired him when Elizabeth disappeared. That's pretty much it."

Terry took a slow sip and placed the coffee on the table. "Why is he still here? She's not missing anymore. The doc should have paid up by now." He leaned in. "So, where's Ross?"

Careful, Amanda. "He fell in his apartment, tripped over a rug, broke an ankle. They're visiting him."

"Really? I don't recall a rug in his place."

She froze. *Shit.*

"One more chance. Or." He stared down at his coffee cup again. "We will have a problem." He turned around to check his surroundings.

Amanda grabbed his cup, and when he turned back to her, she tossed the hot liquid in his face.

He screamed.

She ran.

"Nick!" Elizabeth ran over to him, her arms extended. He was sitting on the side of his bed, looking pale and out of it. She sat beside him and held him tight.

At first, he didn't respond. But then he blinked. She called his name again and said, "It's me, Elizabeth."

He blinked into her smile. "Elizabeth?" His voice was weak.

"It's really me, Nick."

Her arms wrapped around him, and he held her back. Not tight, more resting.

"I missed you. I know it was only one night, but I haven't stopped thinking of you."

Powers had placed Nick on an antidepressant to help him lose the fog in his head. It appeared to have worked.

Nick caressed her hair. "I was so worried. It was all my fault for leaving you."

She pressed a finger to his lips. "It wasn't you, I swear. We need you to get better, and..." She didn't know how to continue. She only knew she was getting him out of the hospital and away from Terry. She looked over at Hank. "Hank will help us."

———

I had placed my phone on mute when I entered the hospital, but felt a vibration in my hand. I told Powers I needed to take the call, and he nodded. Walking out of the room and down the hall, I said, "Amanda?"

"He's after me!"

"Who?"

"At the donut shop, I threw hot coffee in Terry's face."

"Whoa, back up. Where are you now?"

"In the hospital."

"Not Emergency, I hope. That would be the first place he'd run to."

"No, no. The waiting room. I'm scared." She kept rattling on about her encounter, her breathing labored.

"Stay put. I'm on my way."

"That bitch is gonna pay!" Terry stood inside the Holy Donut's men's room, splashing cold water in his eyes.

Sammy, his loyal henchman, stood by the door.

"What do you want me to do?"

"Kill her! My eyes, I wanna rip them out of my head. Hand me some paper towels."

After a few minutes, Terry opened his eyes as wide as possible. "Damn, they're burning like hell."

"We gotta go to the emergency room. It's down the block."

"I know where it is!"

I raced to the waiting room. Amanda had slid in between two people, her eyes watching the door.

I waved, and she charged over to me. "Get me out of here."

"We have to wait for Elizabeth. She's still with Nick."

She held my arm tight. "I did a stupid thing, splashing coffee in his face. He said he'd do the same to me if I didn't answer his questions. I overreacted."

I thought about JR's suggestion. *Have him come after you.* "Okay, grab an Uber and go straight to Elizabeth's motel. We'll catch up soon."

"Hank, Terry must have followed you this morning to her motel. That's how he knew we were here."

"Christ. Okay, go back to the motel, get your car, and find another place to stay. I suspect Terry will be here a while."

Amanda nodded nervously. As we skirted the emergency entrance, I said, "I'll wait until you're safely out of here."

She nodded again, then contacted an Uber.

"A driver should be here in less than five minutes. A white Camry." She shoved her hand in mine like a child and kissed my cheek.

I waited until the driver left the hospital grounds, then walked back to Nick's car. I noticed a black F-150 parked next to his car. I liked it less when I noticed a guy in the driver's seat, his arm extended out the window. No tattoo.

I walked over to the truck and met the guy's face.

"You lost?" I said, with a smirk.

"Shit!" The guy stretched to the glove compartment, but I elbowed his head and he screamed.

"Not smart."

"You bastard! You could've broken my neck. Wait 'til Terry finds out."

"What, that I hurt his little man? He's got more important things on his mind. I think you boys better go back to your car washing business and get rid of your records before the feds raid the place."

He turned his head and grimaced. "You know…?"

"I do now, and Terry won't be happy when he finds out you told me." I grinned.

"I didn't tell you shit." He got in my face. "And don't think Terry's going anywhere without his wife."

"He's gotta know by now she's not interested in being married to him. With his looks, he could get any woman."

"Funny." Sammy looked in his rearview mirror. "Where the hell is he?"

"Getting coffee stains out of his eyes. You might have to drive for a while."

"Who the fuck are you anyway? You ain't the shrink Elizabeth's been sleeping with."

I ignored his question. "You got a name, sport?"

"You tell me yours first." A crooked smile showed a missing incisor.

"I guess Terry doesn't pay for dental care."

His tongue slipped through the missing area. "Fuck you."

"You know, you have a very limited vocabulary."

"F—…wiseass." He grabbed the door handle. I was waiting, hoping he'd step out of the truck. But he held back.

"The name's Hank. What's yours?"

He hesitated. "Sammy."

"Okay, Sammy, we're friends now. Let me give you some friendly advice. If you and your friend don't leave Fort Lauderdale soon, you'll be locked up."

"For what, a broken taillight?" He laughed guardedly.

I walked to the back of the truck, took out my Glock, and with the handle, smashed the left taillight.

"You shit!" He jumped out and paused when he noticed my Glock.

"Shit!"

I smiled. Sammy and I were toe-to-toe. He was younger, but a little on the light side. He looked at the ground where plastic from the taillight accumulated. "What'd you do that for?"

I looked him up and down. He wore ragged jeans and a T-shirt that looked like they hadn't been washed in days. He wore flip-flops, and his ankles were filthy. I almost felt sorry for him.

I pointed at his chest. "You might have connections in your town, but here, you're just another turd passing through. You're in my territory, friend. Like I said, move on."

"You a cop?"

"You're getting warm."

"What the hell does that mean? If you ain't a cop, then what do you do?"

"Undertaker. And I need business. You wanna be a customer?"

Sammy scratched his head. "You're crazy, you know that?" He looked at the broken taillight. "Terry's gonna be pissed."

I broke into his space. "I have a sale on today. Two for the price of one. Same coffin." I winked.

"Crazy."

"Your boss knows where to find me. Tell him I'll be waiting. And one more thing? If you plan on doing something stupid with whatever's in your glove compartment, there are CCTV cameras all over the place." I pointed to one on the hospital wall. "Just reminding you."

I left him scratching his head. Hopefully not head lice.

I hopped into Nick's car, started the engine, and adjusted the rearview mirror. I noticed a guy stepping outside the hospital, a patch over his right eye. I powered the driver's side window and waited until he approached.

Through his good eye he gazed at Sammy, who hadn't moved.

"Sammy's got some advice for you."

Terry jerked his head toward me and glared through his good eye.

"And don't forget to change your eye patch twice a day."

I watched Terry and Sammy leave the hospital parking lot before calling Elizabeth. From the looks of things, they had more pressing things on their minds than following us.

While waiting, I reviewed my encounter with Sammy. By now, he'd be shooting his mouth off about our friendly exchange. That, I was sure, would rile Terry further, and he'd come after me personally. That was my intent anyway. It wasn't likely Terry and company were leaving Fort Lauderdale anytime soon. Nor would I. Not until this Elizabeth business was finally resolved. The problem: would it end peacefully?

Elizabeth appeared and jumped into the front seat—a good sign.

"Thanks for bringing me here to see Nick." She sighed. "He's getting better already." Big smile.

Elizabeth was obviously upbeat. During our visit, while Elizabeth and Nick were sitting together, Doctor Powers had told me he observed Nick making some progress from his breakdown and would like Elizabeth to return as soon as possible. I assured him she would.

I returned her smile, happy for them, but we still had to deal with the husband. Not wanting to spoil her moment, I left Terry out of the conversation.

"I think I'll return tomorrow if that's okay, Hank."

"Of course," I promised, though wondered: didn't Elizabeth realize there were other pressing matters going on in her world?

"Maybe he can be discharged in a few days," she went on.

"Doctor Powers told you this?" I asked, wrinkling my brow.

She buckled her seat belt, then turned to me. "I'm hoping."

Right. And maybe Terry will disappear.

Again, not wanting to spoil her mood, I said, "Great."

I pulled out of the parking lot with no destination in mind. I hoped by now, Amanda had found a new motel, which was fine, because I needed to talk to Elizabeth alone. "How about we go for a ride, get out of here for a few hours?"

"Just the two of us?"

"Why not? Give Amanda a call and tell her we'll meet up with her later."

"Okay."

They spoke a few minutes, Elizabeth doing most of the talking, going on about her visit with Nick. By the sound of the conversation, it appeared to be mostly one way. Finally, she said, "I will. See you later."

She turned to me. "Amanda wasn't in a talkative mood."

"Probably just busy."

"I think she likes you, Hank."

I kept my eyes on the busy road, heading north on Federal Highway. "I like her too."

"I mean, I think she's into you. She finds you attractive. You married?"

Jesus, just what I need right now.

"Divorced."

"Great. She's getting divorced, and so am I. Wouldn't it be cool if the four of us became family?"

Good God, she sounds serious! The woman totally lacked a sense of reality.

"We can talk about it once we clear up the current situation." I felt a headache coming on.

She sighed as though I'd burst her balloon. "Right, Terry. I wish someone would kill him." She turned to me. "Know a good hit man?" She giggled.

I pressed my head. Maybe a migraine. The giggle felt false. For a woman petrified of her husband, she appeared too calm, and I guessed it had to do with her visit with Nick.

"I think we should talk about Terry's business dealings. I'm guessing you know more about his car washing business, maybe even have records showing he's running an illegitimate operation. We could have him arrested."

Elizabeth didn't appear too keen on the idea and crossed her arms. "I'd be better off if he was gone altogether. Know what I mean, Hank?"

Was she seducing me into uncharted waters? Did Elizabeth want the business *all* for herself?

Terry fumed. "You let that bastard break my taillight? The hell, Sammy. Didn't you threaten him with your weapon? Trust me, before he could put a finger on my truck, he'd have six holes in him. You getting soft on me?"

Sammy's hands tightened on the wheel as he drove back to the motel. "I tried reaching for my piece in the glove compartment, but he was too quick. I tell you, Terry, the guy's a nut job. You saw the way he came up to us at the Imax Theater like he didn't have a care in the world."

"Yeah, well, let's see how tough he is when *I* confront him. I know where he's staying. Did the schmuck give you his name?"

"Hank."

"Just Hank. No last name?"

"We only exchanged first names."

Terry cracked up. "You *exchanged* first names? Like what, you're on a first date or something? Did you find out what the guy does for a living, or was that too intimate?"

"Said he was an undertaker."

"Yeah, right."

Sammy stopped at a light. "He sounded truthful."

"He was messing with you, for chrissake!" Terry touched his eye patch and grimaced.

"Think so? He even said he needed the business."

Terry scratched his head. "That's bullshit, and you fell for it. What a dumb-ass. At least we know who he isn't."

"Whatta you mean?"

"For sure, he's not a cop. They ain't supposed to break taillights. We gotta figure out who this wiseass really is and take him down."

"You wanna go to the doc's house now?"

Terry yawned. "Nah, we'll wake him up tonight when he's

asleep. I got that spare key, remember? We'll see who gets the last laugh." He snorted.

Traveling on I-95, they approached a huge highway sign that read: Bush and More Gentleman's Club. It showed a woman halfway up a dancing pole with a cigar in her mouth and wearing a black halter top and matching shorts.

"You see that, Sammy?"

Sammy turned. "Damn."

"I wanna get a lap dance. It'll soothe my eye."

TWENTY-THREE

Driving North on A1A

E lizabeth and I shared small talk, mostly about her growing up as a twin in upstate New York.

"Amanda and I were inseparable. We didn't have many friends, mainly because we just confused people, or they saw us as freaks. Anyway, that was fine. She's my best friend." Elizabeth paused. "I hate putting her through this, Hank." She peered out the window. "I should have listened to her years ago."

"Marrying Terry?"

She nodded. "Amanda could see right through him. She said he had an evil streak and couldn't be trusted." She stopped. "I was young and in love. Like I said, we didn't have many friends, and the boys didn't trust us, thought we'd trick them by changing partners. Not Terry. When he met Amanda, he could tell us apart."

"Really? How'd he figure that out?"

She shrugged. "He said he just could. And he was right. He never mixed us up." She sounded wistful. "Then things changed.

A few years into our marriage, he became abusive—not physically—emotionally. At one point, Terry suggested we have a threesome. I laughed at first, but he was serious. I told Amanda, and she thought he was disgusting." She sighed. "A few months later, she took off to Florida. No reason given, just a change in scenery, she said. Only I knew it had something to do with Terry."

I nodded. "It must have been difficult, her leaving. Like you said, you two were inseparable."

"Sure, it hurt. Still does." Her voice cracked. "Though I'm not sure about Amanda. She still has a lot of anger toward me, Terry, and our town in general. She says she's moved on, but I can see by her stinging comments, she really hasn't." She sighed, stared out the window.

"I couldn't move, not with the car washing business. Besides, Terry flat-out threatened me if I had thoughts of leaving." She turned to me. "As much as I miss her, Amanda did the right thing getting out of town. She hated Terry for what he was doing to me. Eventually, they would have killed each other."

Interesting comment.

I drove past the beach area in Delray. Pedestrians were crossing the busy A1A between bars and restaurants, heading to the expansive, white beach and ocean. Which reminded me, I needed to get a tan before heading home, whenever that was.

"Nice." Elizabeth pointed to the ocean. "I haven't seen waves in years. Not since we took a vacation to California." She sighed.

As we continued north, the Atlantic Ocean on our right, Elizabeth continued watching the waves, the surfers, and the crowd, apparently musing about something, perhaps how she'd love to make Terry disappear.

She took a breath. "Great place to live. Especially in the winter. Beats the cold up north." She appeared mesmerized by the beauty of her surroundings: sunny day in the mid-seventies, the wide sandy beach.

"If only," she breathed.

I'd been watching my surroundings as well, and with no threat of being followed, I asked Elizabeth if she'd like to stop, get her toes wet.

She thought a moment. "Maybe just the toes."

Inside the Bush and More Gentleman's Club

"What's with the patch, sexy?" the college-aged Asian woman asked, dancing to Beyoncé's *Dance for You*.

The guy sporting a dragon tattoo on his arm just gawked up at her. She swung around the pole once more, then stopped.

He blinked, realized she was talking to him. "Hey, you should see the other guy," Terry said with a bit of bravado. "Even with one good eye, I can see your sexy body. Love your long, dark-brown hair, my Asian beauty."

She looked around and strutted over to him. "You noticed," she teased. She was dressed, or rather underdressed, in a pink cage mini dress. Sheer and revealing.

"I know beauty when I see it. And I'm looking at it."

"And with one eye." She smiled.

"What's your name?"

She bent down, pressed her chest high enough to reveal small but lovely cleavage. "Asia."

"Seriously? You from Vietnam?"

She turned up her nose. "Bangkok."

Terry had no idea where that was, but assumed it wasn't in Vietnam.

"So, you want lap dance, sexy?" She turned to Sammy, who

also wore a silly grin. He nodded. She pointed her tiny nose at Sammy. "Your quiet friend, him too."

Terry kept his eyes on the cleavage. "That's why we're here."

Sammy asked, "How much you charge?"

Terry scowled. "You don't ask a reputable woman what she charges." Turning back to Asia, he apologized. "Sorry, my friend here has no class."

"It's just I don't have a lot of money."

Terry shook his head.

She moved closer and smiled. "That okay." She glanced around, then nodded for them to follow her.

"Sale today," she said and led them to the back. When they arrived at a makeshift room, lined with beads for walls, she said, "You first, one-eye."

Terry lifted his half-finished glass of vodka and toasted.

To Sammy, he ordered, "Wait for me here."

Inside, Terry sat back on an old cloth chair, while Asia lowered her top. "I give you best lap dance around. Bangkok style." She smiled seductively, playfully touching her small breasts.

Terry took one last gulp from his glass and went for her.

She slapped his hand. "No touchee. See sign outside? Only look." She continued moving her hips while straddling him.

The Fugees's *Ready or Not* began playing. The pain in Terry's eye had all but disappeared. With his good eye, he stared into the empty glass of vodka. He was feeling loopy, and realized he shouldn't be drinking, not after taking a heavy dose of pain killers. Hell, the doctor had given him ibuprofen. Screw that. He'd taken a few of his own pain killers and not the over-the-counter crap.

Asia's breasts rubbed the scary dragon arm. "You like, Mr. One-Eye?"

Terry watched her pull back slightly, and he nodded as

though in a trance. Must be the booze. The song ended and so did the lap dance. She got up. "You pay now." She put out her hand.

"How about I give you an extra hundred for a happy ending?"

She frowned. "I go to college, make money for tuition. No whore. I don't give endings."

Terry was worked up and didn't like taking no for an answer. Hell, if they danced like that, they did other things.

"Two hundred." By then, he began slurring his words. His head was swimming, but he wanted that fucking happy ending.

He grabbed her hand and placed it on his privates. She snatched it away. "You dog!"

Terry grabbed the top of her shorts and pulled her back to him.

"Help!"

Within seconds, two bulls entered and grabbed him by the arms and dragged him out, his glass smashing on the tile floor.

He tried pulling away. "I'll kick your asses."

Right.

Sammy was back at the stage when he heard the commotion. He caught up with the bouncers and stupidly grabbed one by the shoulder. The guy turned and threw Sammy a punch, knocking him to the ground.

Sammy steadied himself on a chair, snatched a knife from an ankle sheath, and headed toward the bulls. Asia, waiting on the side, rushed in and delivered a kick to his crotch, dropping him like a stone.

The patrons cheered.

The bouncers tossed Terry outside, but not before Asia removed his wallet and counted out a hundred bucks.

Oceanfront Park Beach

I turned into Oceanfront Park Beach in Ocean Ridge, paid the ten-dollar fee, and parked near the boardwalk. Lots of people. Who could blame them for being out in perfect weather?

My cell rang.

JR.

"I have to take this, Elizabeth. I'll catch up with you."

She hesitated.

"It's safe," I assured her.

She nodded and took off, skipping like a child. She kicked off her soft sandals, scooped them up, and ran.

"I was about to leave you a voice message."

"Sorry, I'm here at the beach with Elizabeth."

"Say what?"

"I know, sounds weird. How much time do you have to hear the latest?"

"I'm off today, so you have my full attention."

I gave him the full recap, and JR threw a few expletives as he listened.

"So that's how I wound up here." I looked toward the beach. "You can't ignore the women in bikinis."

"That's my Hank."

"I'm thinking of staying a few days when this is over." *Right. Over.* I watched a flock of gulls flying and smiled. In the distance, the lifeguard's whistle alerted swimmers to move closer to shore. Elizabeth faced the ocean but stood far back from the water's edge.

"I forgot, JR, you called me. Any news on the husband? Please tell me he's wanted somewhere."

"Sorry, Hank, can't say he is. But Terry Bash has a record in his hometown of Miller Falls. Seems he was charged with simple assault, disorderly conduct, and driving under the influence. Not all at once." JR laughed. "Warnings, but no time served. He must have friends."

"Maybe he offers special deals on car washes. What about money laundering from the business? According to Elizabeth's sister, he's definitely into it. Know anyone at DOJ? They handle those cases."

"You wouldn't happen to have the name of the company, would you?"

"I'd have to ask Elizabeth." I scanned the beach a little longer than I wanted. No sign of Elizabeth.

"Could be nothing, JR, but I don't see Elizabeth. Let me call you back."

I disconnected, then ran through the sand, past the lifeguard house, looking down the beach. I checked the water. Small waves lapped the shore. I recalled Elizabeth wearing a floral V-neck blouse and jeans. Jesus, Elizabeth, this was not a time for a disappearing act.

I refused to call out her name with hundreds of people around, so I ran to the restroom. Then I called out. Nothing. I picked up my pace, wiping my forehead, and entered the café.

You're killing me, Elizabeth. Outside the café, I took off for the lifeguard shack. Still nothing. Where was she? I dashed back to the parking lot, pulled out my cell, and punched in her number.

Straight to voice message.

"Where are you?" I asked the air.

I stood by Nick's car. *God, when did the sun become so intense?* I wiped my forehead again. My shirt was soaked.

I called Amanda, told her where I was. "Did she call you?"

"No. What do you mean you're at the beach?"

"Elizabeth wanted to go."

"You're kidding, right? She hates the beach. She almost drowned when we were kids."

"I'll call you back."

I trotted to the parking attendant, showed him my PI business card, and asked if he saw a woman leaving the park on foot. I described Elizabeth.

I got a no. Then he said, "There was an Uber driver. I let him pick up his ride without charging a parking fee."

"An Uber? When?"

"Not more than five minutes ago."

"You sure?"

"Positive. I saw his Uber sign." He pointed to the other side of the parking lot. "A woman, that's all I can tell you. I was too busy checking in cars." He thought a moment, then pointed. "He was heading south."

"What about the car? Do you remember make, model, old, new?"

"Jesus, let me think. Old. Black. Small. I think maybe a Corolla."

"Thanks." I ran for Nick's car and took off. I called Elizabeth again. Another voice message. Then I called Amanda, who picked up on the first ring.

"You find her?"

"I think she took off in an Uber. Why would she do that?"

"I have no idea, Hank. Doesn't make sense."

"I'm heading south. Where do you think she'd go?"

Amanda's voice broke. "Like I said, I have no idea. Oh, no, I forgot to tell her I changed motels."

"Where are you staying now?"

"The Resting Place Inn. On Federal Highway."

"Okay, good, Keep trying her phone."

"Do you think she saw Terry and took off? What if he found her, Hank?"

"Unlikely. I was careful about my surroundings. I have to go, Amanda. And call me if you get in touch with her."

I disconnected and continued a few miles over the speed limit. The last thing I needed was to be stopped.

Up ahead, I noticed a black car and moved quickly to catch up and pulled alongside. The Uber insignia was pasted on the front windshield. The damn windows were too dark to identify the rider. I thought quickly, removed my old detective shield—a big no, no, but I was desperate—then lowered my passenger window, and flashed the almighty shield and got the driver's attention.

The sixty-something-year-old lowered his window and squinted at me, then pulled over in front of a convenience store. I parked behind him and approached his car.

"What's going on, officer?" His face turned white, as though he'd been caught with contraband.

I spied the back seat. The woman asked, "What's wrong?"

She was around twenty, Hispanic, and dressed in shorts and a T-shirt.

"Sorry. I got a call about a possible abduction in a car with your description. You don't look like you're being kidnapped, ma'am."

Her eyes widened. She looked at the driver. "He's Uber."

"I'm Uber," assured the driver. "You have the wrong car."

I looked at him closely, then the rider. "All good. Have a nice day, folks." I watched the car pull out and continue south. I shook my head.

I had a real problem on my hands.

I drove back to the beach entrance and asked the attendant if perhaps another Uber had been contacted for a ride.

He looked at me. "Oh, hi. Yeah, there was another one. Like, maybe ten minutes ago." He pointed south. "Same as the other one."

"What do you mean?" I asked quickly. "The same woman?"

"Huh, no. A woman is what I meant."

My head was spinning. These twins were screwing up my brain.

He said, "I'm guessing the woman in the first car wasn't who you were looking for."

Smart guy. "Unfortunately, no. Can you give me a description of the vehicle?"

A big smile. "Oh yeah. A white BMW X3. I really wasn't paying attention to the plates."

"Wait, you're telling me an Uber driver pulled up in *that* vehicle? That's an expensive car for an Uber driver. You sure?"

"Positive. My son-in-law owns one. I spoke to the guy. He was thirtyish and friendly." He shrugged. "He said he did it for fun. Cool, no?"

No, especially when you can buy an Uber decal sign online for ten bucks.

"Very. And you said they headed south?"

"Right, like the other driver."

I thanked him and left. I headed south again, trying to understand the expensive car thing. I doubted the guy was an Uber driver. I also knew Terry drove an F-150. So, who was the driver? More important, was Elizabeth the rider?

I called Elizabeth, and again, it went straight to voice mail. I pounded the steering wheel. She was definitely pissing me off. I continued south, but I was sure the fancy BMW would be long gone by now. I called Amanda, gave her the latest, and asked if she knew anyone who drove an X3.

"Hank, I don't know what that is."

"A BMW."

"Nope, not familiar. Oh, well."

Oh, well? Her tone turned flat. Heck, if it were my twin, my voice would have cracked like when we spoke before.

"You sound too cool, Amanda. What's going on?"

I got tired of her momentary lapse in conversation and said, "Will I ever get the truth out of you twins?"

"Hank, that's silly. Of course, I'm concerned for Elizabeth. She's my twin sister."

"We both know that, but it feels like you're holding back. Are you, Amanda? Because I can't do my job if you and Elizabeth are toying with me."

She sighed. "I'm just damn tired of what's been going on. I'm truly sorry for you, and especially Nick, getting involved with Elizabeth. She and I are totally different. Yes, we're identical, but that's as far as it goes. I told you, my sister likes bad boys. I don't. When she popped up again after all these years, I tried forgetting the past. But the past followed her down here. I'm rambling. Please find the truth."

TWENTY-FOUR

Terry woke up with a start. Christ, the interior of his truck felt like an oven! His T-shirt was drenched with sweat, so he started the engine and cranked up the A/C, sticking his head in front of the vent.

He rubbed his good eye, then checked his watch. Two p.m. He'd been out for—he couldn't say. And where the hell was Sammy? He glanced around. That shit better not still be inside the strip joint.

The hell happened? Terry's head pounded from the booze or drugs or both. Real stupid. He licked his lips for moisture and realized he had to be dehydrated. Then he recalled being kicked out on his ass, which meant he couldn't go back inside and look for Sammy. So, he called him.

"I'm out fishing…"

He hung up. Stupid message. If that bastard was getting laid—

But then he realized that couldn't happen. They didn't allow it. Terry opened the door and struggled out of the truck. He had to pee badly and took a whiz on the front tire.

"Ah." He zippered up, then returned to the vehicle, but not before checking his wallet.

The bitch had ripped him off a hundred bucks, and he hadn't gotten a happy ending. He shook his head in anger and got dizzy. "Oh, crap." He held onto the car door, but he still felt loopy and didn't move for a while. When he did, Terry called Blade. Another voice message: "I'm not here."

"What the fuck's up with you guys?"

He managed to get back into the truck without falling down and leaned against the steering wheel.

"Screw it! I need to get some sleep." He pulled out of the lot and stayed in the right lane. When he reached his motel, he glanced up at his room. This Elizabeth business was wearing him out. She kept outsmarting him.

"I just need to sleep it off," he mumbled, staggering over to the stairs and holding onto the rail for support, counting the damn steps until he reached the landing.

"Never again," he swore. Looking down at his truck, a thought hit his murky brain: yeah, he wanted her, but hell, he didn't need her to operate the *real* business. He could make lots of money without her.

When he reached the door, he searched his pants pocket for the key card, and after two tries, swiped the door open.

"Christ! That fucking musty smell." He stepped over to the air conditioner, cranked it up, then aimed himself toward the bed. Just before he dropped onto the unmade bed, Terry's thoughts remained constant.

I'm gonna kill that bitch and everyone with her.

And then his phone rang.

Oceanfront Park Beach

Amanda had said, "Please find the truth."

Maybe she already knew the truth. Especially, after this last stunt. My guess: Elizabeth was no longer running *from* Terry.

Damn you, Elizabeth, you're on your own!

I looked out at the ocean. The waves had calmed, producing an almost mirror-like setting. What I could use right now. Breathing in the balmy salt air, common sense told me to get the hell out of Florida.

In spite of Elizabeth taking off, I had accomplished my mission. But I owed it to Nick to explain my decision before heading home. Let him figure out what to do with his perfect woman, assuming he was capable of it, which no doubt, wasn't any time soon.

As I scanned the serene ocean, seagulls squawked and dived at minnows. I'd return for a little R&R another time for sure.

I took a breath before calling JR. "I'm done here," I said, trying to keep my tone even. "There's nothing more I can do, and my expenses are piling up."

It took a few moments for JR to respond. "You sound frustrated."

"Frustrated! She took off again. From *me*! The woman's a total whack job. There's no reason for me to stick around. Once I pay Nick and your aunt a visit, I'm outta here."

JR must have been pondering my decision, so when he held off, I said, "You there?"

"I'm here, Hank. You're right, there's no reason to stick around. I'm hoping Elizabeth will disappear for good. Too bad my cousin fell for her."

Three bikini-clad women strolled by and smiled. I offered one back, then walked under a queen palm for relief from the imposing sun. "I'm sorry about all this, JR. I hope you understand."

"Believe me, I'd do the same if I were in your predicament." He paused. "Could you do me a favor and stay another day, maybe get some sun? I'll catch a flight tonight, or tomorrow morning at the latest. I think it's best if I'm with you when we talk to my aunt. She's up in age, and I know she'll need my support. Then we'll visit Nick."

"Anything for you," I agreed without hesitation. Two more bathing beauties walked past and smiled. Waiting another day wouldn't be so bad. "I'm kinda glad you're coming. It would be nice if we could persuade Terry to leave Fort Lauderdale. I'd feel better about going back home."

"My exact thoughts. I'll call you when I book a flight."

I disconnected and took a breath. I found a towel and blanket in Nick's trunk and headed back to the beach. I drifted to the far side, away from the crowd, spread the blanket, and lied down. As the sun warmed me, and a cool breeze wafted over me, it didn't take long before I drifted off.

My phone trilled from my pants pocket, jolting me from a nap, my eyes opening to the sun. I shielded my face and grabbed the phone.

"Hello." My mouth was dry and my face felt hot, which I was sure I would pay for later.

"Hank, it's Amanda. You sound out of it. Where are you?" Her voice raced on—.

"Whoa, slow down. You're not making sense. What's going on?"

"It's about Elizabeth. She called rambling about Nick and

Terry and about something bad happened. I couldn't understand most of what she was saying. She begged me to call you, said you would know what to do."

I stood and looked around, my head fuzzy from the nap. "How would I know what to do if I don't know where she is? Did she say where she is?"

"She wouldn't say."

I clenched my fist. "Then how the hell am I supposed to help?"

"Call her. Maybe you can make sense of what's going on."

"Damn it, if she had stayed put, we wouldn't be having this conversation."

"I know and I'm sorry. I just didn't know who else to call."

"Okay, stay where you are." I hung up and punched in Elizabeth's number.

Straight to voice mail.

"Call me ASAP," I demanded, then hung up.

I called Amanda back. "She's not answering. What was the gist of the conversation?" I tried keeping my tone even as my frustration mounted.

"She said something about visiting Nick. I thought you guys already saw him today."

"We did. So, why would she return without me? We agreed on visiting Nick tomorrow. What the hell is she up to?"

"You can never tell with her. She's irrational at times."

"Obviously." I squeezed my eyes shut, trying to clear my head, then grabbed the towel and blanket and started for the car. "How the hell can I help if I have no idea where she is?" I stopped. "Wait a second, you said Nick *and* Terry."

"Right."

"Nick's supposed to be in the hospital—"

"Oh, no. You think Elizabeth went to get him out? Why

would she do that? Isn't he sick?" Her voice shot up a few octaves.

"Who knows with Elizabeth? I'll call when I get some news."

"Okay, please hurry."

I hung up. My mind raced, trying to decide what to do next. I checked the time. Christ, I'd been out almost two hours. Anything could have happened in that time.

I jumped in the car and called Doctor Powers. I reached his voicemail. "This is Hank Reed. Urgent."

I left the beach and took the side streets to I-95, then headed south. Coral Springs General was about twenty minutes away, and when I arrived, the parking lot was full.

Damn sick people. I squeezed into the last spot at the edge of the lot and ran inside. Doctor Powers still hadn't returned my call, and that troubled me. When I reached the reception desk, a woman retiree type smiled.

"I need a visitor's pass to see Nick Ross. He's a patient."

Of course he was a patient. Slow down.

While waiting for the pass, I surveyed the area. Standing room only, with chairs arranged in fours, opposite each other, and large screen TVs hanging on the walls like a sports bar. Yet, for a crowded place, it was eerily quiet.

"I'm afraid he's been discharged."

I turned back to her and frowned. "That can't be. I was just here this morning visiting him."

Another quick smile, then back to the computer. "He definitely checked out." The woman offered a sympathetic expression. "Maybe that's a good thing."

Definitely not good.

"When was he discharged? It couldn't have been that long ago."

She sighed. "Sorry, I'm not at liberty to give you that information."

My face burned from the sun, or was it aggravation? "Okay, I need to see Doctor Powers."

Again, at the computer. "He's off today." She caught herself as though she'd violated a privacy rule.

I ran for the exit, almost knocking over a guy on crutches. Elizabeth's crazy message to Amanda now made sense.

TWENTY-FIVE

Back in the car, I called Amanda.

"Nick checked out of the hospital," I said, my tone harsh. "Who do you think assisted him? Let me guess: the same woman who took off on me again. What the hell for?"

"I don't know. I mean, he's sick."

"Of course, he's sick. Apparently, your sister is equally sick, trying a stunt like that. I'm guessing you haven't heard from her."

"Not yet." She stopped. "Oh, God! That's what Elizabeth was mumbling about."

Smart thinking.

"She has to be with Nick."

"And Terry. If you heard right through her gibberish, Terry's with them. Not good, Amanda."

"Maybe he grabbed them right out of the hospital."

"Doubt it. Terry had no idea she'd be there. Hell, neither did I. He obviously found out somehow."

"I hope you're not suggesting I called Terry. That's crazy, I hate the guy. Besides, I thought Elizabeth was with you."

142

She was right, of course. All roads pointed to Elizabeth and her disturbing need to hire a hit man. But Nick?

"Sorry. I didn't mean to imply you were involved in his release, but until I find them, I have no way of knowing if there was foul play."

"We have to call the police," she finally admitted.

"Hold off. I'm heading over to Nick's place now. I'll call you later."

"Okay. And Hank, stay safe."

"I intend to."

I hung up and ran for the car. Heading crosstown, I buzzed JR and told him what I'd found.

"This is crazy! Listen, I'm booked on the six-thirty JetBlue flight tonight. I'll call when I arrive."

I stopped for a red light. "Okay, good." I hung up, dropped the phone on the seat, then squeezed the steering wheel. "Come on!"

When I arrived on Nick's street, the area was cordoned off with ominous yellow crime-scene tape, and patrol and unmarked cars angling about. I found a spot at the beginning of the block and charged for Nick's building. Not good: a fire and rescue vehicle stood in front, lights flashing.

Christ, Terry killed Nick or Elizabeth, or both. I pushed my way to the front of the crowd. "What happened?" I yelled to no one in particular.

"Looks like maybe a murder. Scary."

I pulled out my wallet and held up my expired detective shield before lifting the tape, walking slowly toward a uniform.

"Whoa, you can't come in here." The guy approached me, his hand on his holster. "Even if you live in the building."

"What happened?" I asked, shoving my shield in his face.

He scrutinized it. "You're not from here."

No kidding!

"I'm not in the business anymore, but I am a private investigator and my client lives in that building. I got a call that there might have been foul play."

He studied me a moment. "Hold on." Tall and pale, he looked like he'd recently graduated from the police academy. He called over a suit, a mean-looking African-American guy. He spoke a moment and nodded in my direction.

The detective waved me over. He introduced himself as Detective Walker. "What's this about your client?"

I took a breath. "Nick Ross. Can you tell me if this has anything to do with him?" I handed him my business card and shield. "Look, I know you don't know me, and I don't expect any favors, but I'd like to know if he's okay."

He handed back my shield. "Suffolk County. Interesting. Who would I contact to confirm who you are?"

My heart shifted a beat. I opened my phone and showed him Jimmy Stanton's title and number. "I know stuff and believe I can help you."

Walker said nothing. He took out his phone, made a mental note of Stanton's phone number, and walked a few feet from me. A few minutes later, he said, "Come with me."

I surveyed the crowd, my eyes catching a worried-looking Mrs. Burke with Tiger. She noticed me and offered a nervous wave. I nodded to her.

Inside Nick's building, a half-dozen law enforcement folks were milling around, so Walker brought me over to a quiet corner. I wondered how many other investigators were in whosever unit the crime took place.

He turned to me. "I wouldn't normally do this, but if you have information I need, I'm willing to take a chance. Stanton confirmed that you were former Homicide Detective Hank Reed. He told me to tell you to stay out of trouble." He smiled. "Sounds like it's too late for that."

No funny retorts.

"There's been a murder. Seems your client was the shooter."

"Nick?" My eyebrows furrowed. "That's impossible. I just visited him this morning at Coral Springs General."

"You mean he was a patient?"

Tread lightly, Hank. "As far as I know, he was heavily medicated, so I can't imagine why he was released. Or capable of killing anyone." I paused. "And as far as I know, Nick Ross doesn't own a gun."

Walker mulled over my comments. He finally said, "When we arrived, he was sitting in a chair with a Walther P22 in his hand. He posed no threat to us because his eyes were closed and his body slack."

"Well, there you go. Like I said, he'd been heavily sedated at the hospital. And the way you described his appearance, the killer must have planted the weapon in his hand afterward."

Walker shrugged. "Maybe. My partner is upstairs with him. We'll soon find out."

I asked, "Who's the vic?"

His eyes swept the floor, then to me. "Don't know. He didn't have any ID on him. That's where you might come in handy."

"A he?"

"Right."

"He wouldn't happen to be white, late thirties, with a nasty dragon tattoo on his left arm? And a patch over one eye? Well, maybe the patch is gone by now."

Walker wrinkled his forehead. "So, you do know the guy."

I nodded. "His name is Terry Bash, and he's from Miller Falls, New York. He's in the car washing business, with an emphasis on *wash*." I grinned nervously. "Could be connected to the business."

While Walker took notes, I said, "Look, my client is a well-respected psychologist and doesn't wash cars. He's never had as much as a speeding ticket." I didn't know if that were true, but it sounded good.

He nodded absently, kept writing. "Maybe, but your client must have known the vic. It's too much of a coincidence that he was killed in Ross's apartment."

I ignored his response and explained, "Nick Ross hired me to find someone, and I did."

Walker lifted an eyebrow. "Not the vic, I hope."

"The guy's wife. She was running away from him, only my client didn't know she was married at the time—nor now, for that matter." I crossed my fingers.

More thinking. "Okay, then why are you still here, P.I. Reed? To collect your fee?"

"I decided to stick around since my client isn't well. I owed him that much."

He threw a grin. "Very admirable, but I'm sure there's more to the story."

I took a breath. "Okay, look, Nick met this woman at a local bar last Saturday night—we'll call her Elizabeth. They went back to his place, got romantic, and the next morning when my client went out to bring back breakfast, she vanished."

Walker shook his head. "Come on, that shit happens all the time. This Elizabeth must've realized she wasn't interested and took off while he was gone. That's not a stretch."

I nodded. "I thought so too, at first, but then my client told me about a threatening phone call he received that morning before he went out. My client thought it was a crank call from a friend, but when he returned, she was gone."

Walker began writing furiously as not to miss a beat. I assumed he'd record us instead of taking notes, but hey, the old school must work for him.

When he stopped, he said, "So where's this Elizabeth now? You said you found her afterward."

I told Walker the rest of the story: Nick's breakdown, the hospital, and Elizabeth's final disappearing act. I waited for Walker to finish his note-taking, then said, "Elizabeth has to be involved. If she helped Nick get discharged and return here, she must have had a motive. Maybe she knew the husband would show up and she'd get a chance to kill him."

Walker raised an eyebrow, and I nodded.

"She took off, leaving the weapon in my client's hand."

"Possible."

"And another thing: she asked me if I knew a hit man."

He looked pointedly at me. "You're saying Elizabeth, or whatever her name is, set your client up. They have a romantic evening, she disappears, then reappears, and then this."

"Look, Detective, I know it sounds crazy, but I think she set up my client from the get-go. She must have sensed he was an easy mark, and this is the result of it."

Walker thought a moment. "You're not bullshitting me to go easy on your client, are you, Reed?" He frowned.

"Absolutely not. When I find her—"

Walker put up a hand. "This isn't your case."

"Sorry, I was on the job too long."

Walker studied me. "But…if you do obtain information, I expect you to share it with me. Remember, I'm allowing you here as a professional courtesy."

I nodded. "I want the real killer caught as much as you do, Detective."

"Good, I'm glad we understand each other." He paused. "Why did your client hire a New York P.I.? I'm sure he could have easily found one locally."

"True, but my client is related to a good friend of mine, a *senior* New York City homicide detective. He's actually on his way here as we speak."

Walker kept his gaze on me, then tucked away his notebook. "I want to show you something."

We let a few CSI folks off the elevator before getting on. "Looks like they're done," I observed.

When we arrived at Nick's floor and headed inside, I could hear what sounded like a one-way conversation.

I found Nick in the living room, sitting in a chair, in cuffs. His unfocused eyes stared at the floor while Walker's partner barked questions at him, not that he was getting anywhere. Nick was clearly on another planet.

I looked around for Terry, my eyes stopping at the kitchen floor, where he was sprawled out, his head leaning to one side in a pool of blood. I gathered he'd taken at least one to the head.

The detective interviewing Nick was dressed in street clothes, and when he turned to us, he scowled. "Who the fuck is he?"

Walker thumbed at me. "He's a P.I. Ross hired and a former homicide detective. Name's Hank Reed. All good." Walker turned to me. "Smitty gets that way on the job sometimes." He turned to his partner and cracked a smile. "Meet Detective Smith."

Smith was medium size with short brown hair, in his mid-thirties and sporting a three-day stubble. He stood up and folded his arms. "Yeah, well, I hope you vetted him."

Walker nodded. "I spoke to his former boss. He vouched for him. Reed here was hired by the accused. I think he can help us."

Smith looked at Nick then me. "Yeah, well, your client isn't very chatty today."

I turned to Nick, who wouldn't or couldn't recognize me. He sat slouched, minus the weapon, still unfocused.

"Like I told Detective Walker, I just saw Nick at the hospital this morning. He was out of it, kinda like he is now. He couldn't have managed to get here by himself. He hired me to find a woman, apparently, the same woman who helped him get out of the hospital and bring him back here. I provided your partner with information."

Smith eyed Walker, who nodded. "Like Reed said, the woman helped get him out of the hospital a little while ago."

"You can check with Doctor Martin Powers from Coral Springs General." Powers wasn't in, so I hoped he wouldn't call yet.

Smith seemed to mull over my response. "And the dead guy inside, who's he?"

"The missing woman's husband. Detective Walker can fill you in on the details, but my client hired me to find the wife— though he didn't know she was married. They became an item and then she disappeared." I stepped carefully over to Terry, looked down. His dragon was as dead as he was. "That's the husband, all right. A nasty guy who chased her from upstate New York. He intended to bring her back one way or another." I turned to Smith. "Guess that won't be happening."

Smith rubbed his stubble. "So, she and your client hooked up and the husband winds up murdered in his apartment?"

"Like I said, my client didn't know she was married at the time." I glanced over at Nick. "I doubt he knows it now. Look at him. I'm sure if he knew, he wouldn't have been interested."

"Why not? People get involved with married people all the time. Well, maybe not me." He gave me a smirk.

I ignored his sarcasm. "I can't tell you how the husband originally found out she was here, but while my client was out of the apartment, the deceased snatched her. She later escaped." I looked over at Terry. "I guess he got lucky and found her again. Well, maybe not lucky for him." I shrugged.

"Right, lucky. And the woman disappeared again."

"Apparently, soon after the murder. That's why I believe she's the shooter."

Smith challenged, "Says you."

"Look, you know I was a homicide detective before this gig. This whole scene smells like a setup. The woman in question was in a dubious business with the vic here. She wanted the guy dead. Hell, she asked me if I knew a hit man." My eyes shifted from Smith to Walker. "I'm convinced she set up my client."

Walker said, "I think Reed can help us, Smitty."

Smith shot him a look, then to me, said, "Be my guest."

I stood in front of Nick. He didn't blink, nor was he in a talkative mood, and remained still, almost catatonic, and oblivious to his surroundings. My fear was the detectives, more so Smith, wanted to get this case over with, even if it meant arresting Nick prematurely. I was determined not to let that happen, which meant I had to find Elizabeth, and quick.

To appease the detectives, I mentioned I'd be available if they needed me. Since I was technically still on the job—finding Elizabeth again—I'd keep them in the loop.

Walker was okay with it, but his partner was more possessive of *his* case and said he'd be in touch with me if he needed my help. Evidently, Smith was the detective in charge.

"Sure. Your partner has my card."

TWENTY-SIX

I stood outside Nick's apartment complex watching a few stragglers from the crime scene waiting with anticipation of seeing the accused, or more morbidly, the black bag carrying the deceased.

Great entertainment for the day.

Mrs. Burke remained, holding Tiger in her arms. She eyed me and tilted her head in one direction. I sensed Nick's neighbor wanted to talk as she edged away from the crowd.

I crossed the street and followed her to where she stopped in between two apartment buildings.

"Hi," I said, catching up to her. "You probably want to know what's going on——"

She put Tiger down and held the leash tightly. "I heard Nick was in the hospital." She pointed to his building. "What's that all about?"

I peered down at Tiger, who lay on the grass looking bored, then back to the owner. "I can't really say, except they think Nick killed someone. I don't, and I'm working to find out who the real killer is."

"You a cop?"

I didn't want to acknowledge that Nick had hired me, so I said, "Former detective. I'm Nick's friend."

Her eyes shifted back to the crime scene. "A shame. Nick wouldn't hurt a fly. It had to be someone else. Maybe it was *her*." She scowled, letting me absorb her comment.

My eyes widened. "Who?"

She bent down to pet Tiger, who licked her hand. When she peered up, she told me, "I shouldn't be speculating."

"Mrs. Burke, if you have information, no matter how insignificant, the police need to know. Sometimes small details can be very helpful."

Her silence told me she was struggling. "My husband was a police officer, back in New Jersey. He said the same thing. I miss him—my Buddy." She sighed. "He died a few years ago."

I didn't want to appear insensitive. "Sorry for your loss. Buddy was right, so if you can help the police—me—you might get Nick out of a jam."

She sighed again, longer this time.

"A woman." She pointed at Nick's apartment. "It was quick, so I didn't get a good description. She seemed to be in a hurry and ran to a car across the street. She didn't even look while crossing." Her eyes drifted back toward Nick's building. "I watched her jump in the back seat of a car. Buddy would have said she looked suspicious."

Buddy would be right. "And you're sure it was a woman?"

She nodded. "She had the shape of a woman, anyway. Know what I mean? Slim. And her movement as she ran. You can tell, right?"

I supposed so, and I hoped Mrs. Burke could too. "Can you give me a better description?" I asked, my excitement mounting. "This is very important."

Her eyes closed momentarily. "Young—well, everyone is

young to me. She was wearing a ball cap of some kind, and sunglasses."

"Tall, short?"

"Average, for a girl—a woman."

"When was this?"

"I don't remember, but way before the cops arrived."

"You're sure of this?"

"I remember because it was the end of Tiger's routine walk." She pointed to the last building on the block near Nick's condo. "We were about to return when the sirens became louder, scaring the hell out of my poor Tiger."

I looked down at her pooch. He was lying comfortably on his back, legs spread. I almost laughed.

"One more question, and this is crucial. Did you notice the type of car she hopped into? And the color?" I held off asking if she noticed the plate number.

She sighed. "I'm not good with cars, and it took off quickly, but it was big and white, and fancy. Oh, and it didn't have a Florida license plate. It was like an orange gold."

New York?

Her eyes locked on mine. "It might not mean much, but there was a sticker of some kind on the front windshield."

"Decal? Like a business sign? A "U" maybe?"

She shrugged. "Like I said, he pulled out quickly."

"A man?"

She shrugged again. "I'm just assuming. Could have been a woman."

"Mrs. Burke, you need to talk to the detectives working the case. They'd be very interested in hearing what you have to tell them. And don't forget to give them the description of the car— and the plate color."

She seemed to hesitate.

"It's very important and will help Nick. And Buddy would be proud of your observation techniques."

She liked that. "Okay, I can do it."

"The detective's name is Walker. A nice guy. Ready?"

She scooped up Tiger and followed me over to Nick's building. "This is exciting."

Right.

I found Walker in the lobby and introduced him to Mrs. Burke and Tiger. He nodded at both.

"She witnessed something."

I left and headed back to the car. Two questions ran through my head: who had called the cops soon after the murder? And did Mrs. Burke notice if what she saw was an Uber decal?

Back in the car, I called JR. He picked up on the second ring, and I could tell from the background noise, he was still at LaGuardia Airport.

"Hank, there's been a delay, maybe another half-hour."

"Nick's in trouble! He's accused of killing Elizabeth's husband. I just left the crime scene."

"Hold on, it's noisy in here." A moment later. "What's this about Nick in trouble?"

I broke the news, starting with Elizabeth springing Nick from the hospital. When I finished, I waited for JR to respond.

"This is a lot to take in. Something doesn't add up."

"And now she's gone again, and Nick's been arrested. It's hard not to believe Elizabeth set Nick up."

"To kill the husband? I wonder how long she planned that out."

"I'm hoping to have more information by the time you arrive. And JR, Nick's gonna need an attorney."

"Right, of course. I'll make a few calls. He should have one before I arrive. See you later."

I hung up and called Amanda. "Where's Elizabeth? And don't tell me you don't know."

"Hank, I swear, I have no idea where she is. What happened?"

"Terry's dead."

When she didn't answer, I said, "Did you hear me? Your brother-in-law was killed in Nick's apartment. And Elizabeth's missing. Can you explain that?"

"Hank, please, you have to believe me, I had no idea. What about Nick? Is he okay?"

"Why do you ask?"

"I don't know. I just assumed he was with my sister, and if what you say is true, that she disappeared…look, it was an innocent question."

"Nick's been accused of shooting Terry. It happened soon after Elizabeth sprung Nick from the hospital. He doesn't own a gun, and even if he did, in his condition, he wouldn't know which end of the barrel was up."

She mumbled to herself, then said, "Hank, where would my sister get a gun? She certainly didn't have one when she arrived in Florida. Could be someone else killed Terry. Maybe she hired that crazy sidekick of his, Sammy."

Sammy had reached for his weapon in the glove compartment when I confronted him.

"She'd still be an accessory."

"I guess."

She'd guess?

"What do you know about Sammy? He seems to go everywhere with Terry."

"The guy's a creep. He threatened me in *my* house, imitating Terry, saying there would be consequences if I held back sharing where my sister was. I don't think he's smart enough to use the word consequences, but he was still threatening."

"What would he have to gain by killing Terry?"

Amanda held off a moment. "I hate to say this, but maybe Elizabeth offered him a piece of the carwash business in return? Quid pro quo."

Definitely guilty.

"How would she get in touch with Sammy? Especially, considering he was always with Terry?"

"Hank, I'm not a PI. But it wouldn't surprise me if she found a way." Amanda stopped. "I'm sorry, I didn't mean that. I don't think she would hire someone to kill Terry. I mean, she could have had him killed before she ran away from him."

I didn't mention Elizabeth's inquiry of a hit man. Maybe she did seek out Sammy. "If she contacts you, call me."

"Of course."

I hung up. Not expecting JR for at least three hours, and with no place in mind, I decided to surprise Amanda at her motel. Who knows? Maybe I'd find Elizabeth there.

Dusk had settled in. I parked and glanced up at Amanda's motel room. The light was on, and I wondered if she was alone. She'd resent me for not calling in advance, but I wasn't out to make friends, so I'd apologize later.

I paused and placed my ear to the door. Quiet. Maybe too quiet. No TV or radio playing. Several light taps went nowhere. I knocked harder, still, no answer.

Not good! I turned and looked down at the dark parking lot. It was quiet. I knocked one last time, and was about to call her, when the door opened. Amanda stood wrapped only in a towel.

Her glistening hair framed her neck, accenting her beautiful face, and I knew I had made a mistake by not calling first. Or had I?

"Hank, what are you doing here?" Her lips tweaked into a whimsical smile.

"Amanda, I apologize for showing up before calling." I realized she must have just taken a shower. My eyes swept over her, the curve of her breasts protruding above the towel.

"I had no place to go—"

She pulled me inside.

TWENTY-SEVEN

At first, I didn't realize my cell had rung. It was muffled in my pants pocket, which lay near the door where I'd left it. I started for it, but Amanda caught my arm.

"Do you have to?"

What I wanted was to make love again, but that nagging buzzing brought me back to reality.

I leaned over and kissed her on the lips. "Might be important." I kissed her again, then slid out of bed, swearing softly.

I struggled to remove the phone from my pocket.

"Hello." My labored voice must have sounded like I was out of breath.

"Amigo, either I woke you up or you got lucky." JR laughed.

"You're at the airport!"

"I am, and you're not. That's okay; I can take a taxi."

"Wait, I'm less than thirty minutes out," I said, slipping on my pants, then realizing I forgot my Jockeys.

"You sound like you're up to something. Maybe—"

"Be there in thirty."

I hung up and looked back at Amanda, who had an impish grin. She held up my shorts. "You might need these."

"Right." I ran over, and she drew me in and whispered, "We've been going through a lot lately, Hank. I don't regret this. I hope you're not…"

I kissed her tenderly. I thought about asking if she'd see me again, but that was dumb. Of course, she would, one way or another.

I grabbed my shorts, finished dressing, and headed for the door. I turned to meet her eyes. "I'll call you soon."

She gave me a devilish look. "I sure hope so."

Heading out of the parking lot, I felt upbeat. Amanda was beautiful, tender, and loving. Just what I needed at the moment.

JR lingered in front of the JetBlue arrivals terminal, dressed in jeans and a casual blue shirt. As I pulled closer to the sidewalk, I lowered the passenger window and honked. He waved, tossed his carry-on in the back seat, and jumped in the front.

"Hank, you son-of-a-gun, how the hell are you?" He gave me a friendly tap to my shoulder.

My buddy's pale face reminded me of winters up north. He sported a short beard.

I returned the tap and grinned. "Better, now that you're here. I like the new look."

He rubbed his chin. "Yeah, it keeps me warm."

As I pulled away, he said, "I can't stop thinking about Nick. An ordinary guy getting caught up in this…hell?" He shook his head. "I found him a lawyer, supposedly one of the best criminal attorneys in South Florida."

I turned slightly. "He's facing a murder rap, so he'll need a good one." I circled on the terminal exit road and headed toward the Interstate.

JR sighed. "This is gonna kill my aunt. I called her before I left, told her I was taking a mini-vacation and would visit in a day or two. She's worried sick about Nick being in the hospital and frustrated, not knowing what to do for him." He paused. "She didn't mention anything about him getting arrested for murder, which I find strange. I mean, she has to watch some news."

"Maybe it's a blessing for now."

"Not good, Hank. Not good at all."

"You know he won't get bail. Not for murder. Once they pump him full of meds and get him on track, he'll be transferred to a county jail cell."

"Unless we find the killer first."

I said, "Looking back, I wish Nick had been Baker Acted when they brought him in from the beach."

"What's that?"

"It's a Florida law that deals with mental illness. If a person's a danger to themselves or someone else, they can be held involuntarily up to seventy-two hours in a mental health facility." I half-turned to JR. "In Nick's case, he would have been safer in the hospital. What I'm saying is this whole setup wouldn't have taken place, meaning no trumped-up charges against him."

"True, but he wasn't Baker Acted. Let's hope his attorney can persuade the judge to keep him in the hospital," he said glumly. "Except...the judge might wonder why his doctor allowed him to leave in the first place. Sorry, devil's advocate."

I nodded. "Let's hope the devil is wrong." I then asked about the photo I'd texted him, the one of Nick's fishing buddy. "Does your aunt know the guy?"

"Oh, right. She said he really wasn't a friend. And as far as she knows, he's dead."

"Dead? Did she say what happened to the guy?"

"No, and I didn't pursue. Too bad, he might have been helpful."

I recalled viewing the photos. They looked friendly enough to me. Oh, well.

JR removed a Fly Higher cocktail napkin from his back pocket. "The attorney's name is Charles Wilson. He has a practice in Boca Raton. A buddy of mine recommended him. Says he's one imposing big teddy bear until he's in a courtroom. I called him before I left New York. He said he'd heard about the arrest from an online news source and would call the court."

"I know it's late, but how about we call him?"

JR took out his phone and punched in the number. Wilson picked it up on the first ring.

"Yes?"

"Mr. Wilson, this is JR Greco, Nick Ross's cousin. We spoke before. I'm sorry to call this late, but I just arrived in Fort Lauderdale. I'm in the car with Hank Reed, the private investigator I told you about, and we're on speaker. Can you give me an update?"

Wilson came in loud and clear. "Sure, and I go by Charles. You caught me in the tub."

I turned to JR and suppressed a laugh.

"Hold on while I grab a pen and pad."

I swore I heard splashing in the background. I turned to JR and shrugged.

"That's better. Nick was arrested, and booked, but under the circumstances, being that he was incoherent and in need of medical attention, they brought him back to Coral Springs General for observation. I got to see him for less than five minutes, and during that period, Nick was totally unaware of his surroundings."

Wilson went on, "Hank, tell me if I got the timeline right. From what JR told me earlier, this Elizabeth Bash person—the one Nick hired you to find, went to the hospital today and brought Nick back to his apartment. Sometime afterward, the husband showed up, and at some point after that, he was killed. The husband, that is."

"It appears that way. When the police arrived at the crime scene, they found Nick sitting in a chair with the murder weapon in his hands. When I arrived, I persuaded one of the detectives to let me see him. They couldn't get anything out of him. He just sat in some trance-like state. I'd seen it once before with him."

"Interesting." Wilson seemed to have shifted in the tub, causing a slight splash. "Hold on; I'm writing this down."

I smiled to myself and continued, "A witness noticed a woman running from Nick's building—presumably Elizabeth, because she wasn't in the apartment when the police arrived. And according to the same witness, the woman jumped into a big, white, and fancy car, but she didn't get the plate number, only the color."

"The color of the plate?"

"Could be New York. The detectives are working that angle."

"New York. Interesting." Wilson thought a moment. "So, we have Elizabeth and the driver as persons of interest."

"Looks that way. That's all I can offer at this time," I said.

I heard water splashing in the background, and I assumed Charles Wilson was exiting his sacred tub.

"Okay then, we have our work cut out for us. Let's chat tomorrow."

———

JR turned to me, and we broke out laughing.

I said, "Can you just see Charles-the-teddy-bear-Wilson taking notes, bare assed in a bubble bath?"

"I prefer sharing my tub with someone who'll wash my back."

We roared.

It was close to midnight, and too late to visit JR's aunt, so we decided to go for a few drinks.

"You know a place around here?"

I nodded. "Courtney's. That's where Nick and Elizabeth met."

TWENTY-EIGHT

Nick's apartment was no longer a crime scene, so we decided to stay the night. But the next morning, after battling a headache and trying to clear my head from the booze, I popped two Tylenol capsules I'd found in Nick's medicine cabinet in my mouth.

"I could use a few of those myself."

I handed JR the last two, and soon after, we were out the door, heading to his aunt's house.

JR's aunt lived less than a mile from Nick's apartment, in a retirement community called Always Summer. After answering a few questions from the gate guard and getting an okay via a phone call to the aunt, we drove to her unit. The grounds were immaculate. We passed a community pool and tennis courts, both busy.

"I might consider one of these when I retire," JR said, then grinned. "Maybe set up my own Senior Sex Academy."

"You need some R&R, my friend. The cold weather has frosted your brain. Maybe after we solve this case, we'll both take a vacation."

I parked the car in front of unit #450 and got out. JR held off a moment before getting out of the car.

"You okay?"

"Not really. Like I said, this is going to kill my aunt. I'm glad you're with me, Hank. I'm not good at this stuff with relatives."

We followed the short walkway, and about halfway to the door, it opened wide.

"Junior!" called out a spry seventy-something-year-old who hustled over to us. She gave him a hug and kiss, and he reciprocated.

He turned to me. "Aunt Angie, this is my good friend, Hank, Nick's PI."

She greeted me in the same manner: a hug and kiss on the cheek. She took my hand and thanked me for everything. I smiled wistfully. Aunt Angie was an attractive woman wearing little makeup. Her hair was cut in a short, layered bob. "I'm so happy you came, Junior. How's your mother?"

"I told her I was flying down to see you. She sends her love."

"She's my favorite sister, you know."

He smiled. "I believe my mother is your only sister."

She returned the smile, then must have realized the real reason for JR's visit. Her lips turned downward. "Have you seen Nick yet?"

He eyed me then said, "Not yet. I thought I'd visit you first."

Her eyes shifted from JR—who was now Junior, to me. "Come inside; I made muffins."

"Junior," I teased, following him inside.

He jabbed me in the ribs. "Our secret, Hank."

"Sure, *Junior*."

The muffins were warm and filled with blueberries. As we drank coffee and filled our stomachs, his aunt placed several muffins in a brown bag to take along with us. *Thank you, Aunt Angie.*

I could see she was eager to talk about Nick, and we encouraged her. She told us about her only son, stuff JR admitted he'd never known. His aunt was in a talkative yet nervous mood. She told us about his marriage, the car accident, and how he lost his wife and baby, leaving out the juicy parts.

"Nick was depressed for a while, even before the accident—he never mentioned why, and I never pressured him. He started taking anti-depressants. He said he needed to be present for his patients." She paused, stared at the floor before continuing. "If only I'd known, maybe I could have helped him." She smiled sadly. "I guess that's a mother talking." She looked over at us and sighed.

"And then one of his patients killed herself soon after a therapy session." She counted on her fingers. "Wife and child killed in the accident, a patient's suicide, and whatever else he was holding inside him. It was too much. After that, Nick pretty much stopped seeing patients, and soon after, admitted himself into the hospital for exhaustion."

Right, exhaustion. Aunt Angie was being kind.

She sipped coffee, played with the muffin crumbs, and remained silent. She was obviously holding back, but further questioning made no sense at this point.

"Anyway, all those events added to…whatever was going on in his head." She sighed then looked at us. "And now this thing with a woman he just met. It's been horrible."

We both nodded. I wanted to assure her things would get better, that Nick's life would turn around, but I couldn't promise her anything.

She continued, "Another loss. He didn't offer much except to say he had met the love of his life. And then she disappeared. He said they really connected, and he was certain something had happened to…Elizabeth."

I didn't want to tell Aunt Angie that Elizabeth had returned, killed her husband, then set Nick up. That would tear her apart, and I hoped JR would hold off telling her about the arrest.

She started tearing, plucked a tissue from her blue cotton apron that read, 'I'm in Charge Here,' and dotted her eyes. "Sorry."

JR went to her, held her. It was a soft side I'd never witnessed in him. He obviously was fond of his aunt, and when he gazed back at me, his expression was clear.

We need to fix this.

I nodded.

JR remained silent until we returned to the car. "This is very sad. So many misfortunes happening to one person in a short period of time. Hell, I'd have had a breakdown myself." He looked back at his aunt's house. She stood at the window, waving with effort. He waved back.

I said, "Let's go visit Nick's doctor." I pulled out, and after passing the guard house, followed local streets to the Interstate. JR was uncharacteristically quiet. He finally turned to me.

"What do you think about this?"

What did I think? I shrugged. "Nick's been through a lot of emotional pain, and he shut down."

"I know that, Hank. But you saw him last. Is he capable of murder?"

I entered the interstate. "Like I told you on the phone, Nick acted strange the minute I met him. I assumed he had a lot on his mind, but later that day, he went into some sort of mental disappearing act. So, no, I can't believe Nick's capable of killing anyone, especially since he was so heavily medicated when the killing took place. Hell, he could barely sit up."

I exited at Atlantic Boulevard and continued to Coral Springs, which was about fifteen miles from the Fort Lauderdale strip. Unlike beach pedestrians, folks here didn't appear to be in a hurry to cross the street unless they were heading to a Publix supermarket.

When we arrived at the hospital, I punched in Powers's number.

He picked up immediately.

"Hello, doctor, it's Hank Reed."

When he didn't respond immediately, I said, "You there?"

"Yes, sorry. I've been so concerned about Nick, and when I heard your voice…Hank, I'm so worried. They're saying Nick killed someone. That's impossible."

"I'm outside the hospital. We need to talk."

"Yes, of course. Come inside. I'll inform the front desk that I'm expecting you." He hung up.

I turned to JR. "He's not taking it very well."

We met Powers inside his office. I introduced him to JR. They shook hands quickly, and then he motioned us to sit. He settled at his desk, then wiped his brow.

"Hank, I don't understand what happened. I'd taken most of the day off—an emergency—and when I returned that night, Nick was gone." He shook his head. "He discharged himself, which he could because he wasn't under a court order to stay. I didn't think he was capable of making that decision by himself."

"Looks like he might have had help," I said.

He sighed, then nodded. "I hate to say it, but it could have been Elizabeth. A staff member tried calling me but, like I said, I had an emergency and didn't pick up for anyone. My wife…" He gave us a long look, hoping we wouldn't pursue a line of questioning.

JR said, "And this staff member, he was sure the woman was Elizabeth?"

"A she, yes, because Elizabeth had been here before." He turned to me. "With you."

"And she just let him go?" I asked.

Another wipe across the forehead. "We couldn't hold him if we wanted to. Apparently, Elizabeth was very persuasive and told Judy—my staff member—that she would make an appointment with me in a day or two. A follow-up. Look, had I been here, I would have strongly discouraged him leaving, but even that might not have worked." Powers searched my face for encouragement.

I didn't provide any.

He turned to JR. "I'm glad the police realized Nick was too ill to be placed in a jail cell, at least for now. He belongs here where he can get help. I pray they find the real killer quickly." He searched our expression, which must have shown relief. "When Nick arrived, he was rambling about nothing, so I gave him a shot of Haldol, and he went to sleep soon after. Quite honestly, I have no idea what to expect when he wakes up."

"It's obvious my cousin wasn't capable of killing anyone. You know that, Doctor."

Powers responded, "I wasn't at the scene, but from my prior sessions with him, I can't imagine Nick would hurt anyone, let alone fire a weapon. I can only speculate that someone placed the gun in his hand afterward. You don't have to be a professional to think the guy—they said it was a guy—would have acted faster and overpowered Nick."

"I agree," JR said. "I hope you told the cops that."

"Of course. I spoke to a Detective Walker, I believe that was his name, and got the impression he realized it too. As for his partner, he seemed more interested in getting the case over with."

I described Detective Smith.

He nodded. "Him. The guy was an arrogant SOB. Sorry. He thought my evaluation was wrong. At least his partner was more civil and leaned toward my observation."

JR said, "Please update us with Nick's condition."

"Of course. They placed a uniformed policeman outside his door, so I have no authority to let you see him." He shook his head in defeat. "I'm really sorry about this. I need to bring Nick back to health." He then asked, "What about Elizabeth? Was she part of the shooting?"

I side-glanced at JR and then to Powers. "We'll let you know when we find her."

TWENTY-NINE

Outside the hospital, I said, "Detective Walker told me he was putting out an APB on Elizabeth. She's obviously not running away from Terry anymore, but if she had anything to do with his murder, she'd be on the run. My question again is why would she set Nick up?"

"I don't have an answer, Hank. And we won't know until we find her." He paused. "You mentioned Terry's sidekick. Sammy. How can we find him?"

I shrugged. "I don't even know his last name——" I stopped.

"What?"

"Terry's truck. That's where Sammy was going for his weapon when I confronted him. Who knows what else we might find in the glove compartment?"

"Okay, but where's the truck?"

I smiled. "If Terry was going to confront Nick, he'd need transportation."

We hopped in the car, and when I reached Nick's block, I slowed down. "Look for a black Ford F-150."

"What if Sammy took it?"

"Let's hope not."

Halfway down the street, JR pointed. "What about that one? Same color anyway."

I stopped next to the truck. Luckily, I'd memorized Terry's plate number when I confronted them in Fort Lauderdale. I then noticed the broken taillight. "That's it." I double-parked and put on my emergency flasher.

JR asked, "Does your detective friend know about the truck? He had to figure Terry arrived in a vehicle."

"If he did, he didn't mention it. And neither did I." I removed my phone from the console. "What do you think?"

JR put his hand on my shoulder. "Let's hold off calling him."

We shared glances and I nodded. I opened Nick's glove compartment and removed a few napkins.

"I see my cousin likes McDonald's."

I handed him a few. "Who doesn't? "I'll check the driver's side door."

JR walked around the truck to the passenger side and peeked inside. I met his stare from my side, and we smiled at each other.

My door was locked, but JR's was opened, so he reached across, McDonald's napkin in hand, and opened my side.

We surveyed the interior. The back seat was strewn with dirty shorts and T-shirts.

"What pigs! I'd need a tetanus shot if I touched those."

JR reached for the glove compartment. "Bingo." He removed a 9mm by the barrel, took a whiff, then held it up. "Hasn't been fired lately."

"See what other goodies are in there."

JR passed me the gun, then poked around and pulled out a vehicle registration certificate.

He held it up. "Terry Bash, from Miller Falls, New York."

"Past tense. Anything else?"

JR dug around. "Just papers." He was about to shove them back when a credit card dropped onto his lap.

"What the hell."

"What?"

JR held it up. "Must be Christmas in January, Hank. I can't believe the guy was stupid enough to leave a credit card in the glove compartment." He smiled. "The idiot's name is Sam Bison."

"Sammy, Terry's sidekick. Any address?"

JR looked further. "Nope. Maybe Detective Walker can help us out. We don't have to tell him how we found his name."

I handed him back the 9mm. "I'm assuming this gun belongs to Sammy, which makes sense. Terry would have brought his own weapon to Nick's place. I guarantee ballistics will match the gun found on Nick with that belonging to the vic, so it'll look like Nick grabbed the gun from Terry and killed him. Highly unlikely."

"Meaning the shooter brought his own gun."

"Or hers," I added. "Terry wasn't about to hand over his weapon unless someone had another one pointed at him. Maybe someone he wouldn't expect."

"Like Sammy."

I shrugged. "Elizabeth might have sweet-talked him into becoming her new business partner. Assuming she was able to locate him alone."

"Well, Hank, it looks like we need to find Sammy."

I peered out the windshield. "In the meantime, let's give Detective Walker a gift." I made a call and asked Walker to meet us by Terry's truck, which we found by accident.

"It's parked on Nick's block. We'll be here."

Walker said, "Did you call before or *after* you entered the vehicle?" He laughed. "Forget it; I don't wanna know. Be there in fifteen minutes."

I then called Amanda. I'd been thinking about her since I left her and stepped out of earshot from JR.

"Hey," I said. "How are you? Any buyer's remorse from last night?"

She laughed lightly. "Not on my end. You?"

I walked a little farther away from my buddy. "None here."

"Does that mean we're an item, Detective Emeritus Reed?"

"I don't know," I said innocently. "It usually takes a while to get to know someone. But I'd like to continue."

"Me too. I'm checking out of this rat hole now that Terry's no longer a threat. The next time you call, I'll be home, probably preparing a bath. Interested?"

"In a bath? Always." I turned to JR, who also was on the phone. His expression was serious, so I doubted he was talking about sharing a bath.

Amanda said, "My sister hasn't called, and I'm afraid if she was involved in Terry's murder, I might not ever see her again."

"She'll contact you at some point," I encouraged.

"Not if she's running away from a murder," she countered bluntly.

Amanda was probably right.

I changed the subject and said, "How about you call me later when you're settled in?"

"Before or after running the water?" she said, suddenly upbeat.

"Don't tempt me. See you later." I hung up. JR was still on the phone when Detective Walker pulled up behind Nick's car and got out. He was alone, so I didn't have to deal with his asshole partner.

"Hank." We shook hands. JR hung up, and I introduced the detectives. Walker said, "Sorry about your cousin. From one detective to another, I have my doubts he killed the guy, but I need to follow up just the same. I hope you understand."

JR nodded. "I have faith in the system."

Walker pointed. "That the vehicle?"

I nodded. "I noticed it when I arrived at Nick's place. I told you I met the deceased and his partner previously and took down the plate number. I got lucky, I guess."

"It sure looks that way. We would have found it sooner or later, but thanks. Turns out, the deceased had a rap sheet, nothing major, and never did time."

"What about his carwash business? He liked to wash *money* as well."

"I checked with the Miller Falls police chief. He told me there'd been rumors. And since money laundering is a Federal crime, he suggested I call the FBI." Walker paused. "He made sure to tell me he wasn't sad to see Terry Bash leave this Earth."

Walker removed a pair of latex gloves from a jacket pocket and opened the passenger side door.

"It's not locked."

He glanced over at us and mumbled to himself. He kept the driver's side door open, opened the glove compartment, and removed the pistol. He took a whiff. "Hasn't been fired."

I stuck my head inside. "It belongs to a Sam Bison, the victim's sidekick."

Walker took another whiff then turned his head at me. "You know this how?"

"He was going to use it on me once. I persuaded him not to."

"Right. Well, it's not the murder weapon."

I said, "Detective, I think Sammy Bison can help us."

"Yeah, how's that?"

"He knows stuff. He wouldn't go anywhere without Terry. Besides, they only had one vehicle between them."

Walker held the weapon between his fingers. "You said he was the sidekick. Where do you think he went?"

JR chimed, "Depends on whether he helped in the murder."

"You're saying he'd kill his buddy? Why?"

"Money," I added without hesitation.

"Wait here." Walker walked back to his car and returned five minutes later. "Sam Bison has an alibi. He's sitting in the Broward County jail. He was arrested for attacking a bouncer at some topless joint. I guess he got more action than he bargained for." He snorted. "Anyway, he couldn't come up with the bail money."

"I guess we can strike him off our suspect list." I side-glanced at JR. "That leaves Elizabeth Bash as our main suspect."

"Wrong, Hank. You're not part of the investigation. But I agree, it would appear so. We'll find out eventually."

I recalled Amanda telling me I might not see Elizabeth again. "Good luck."

Walker made a call to have Terry's car impounded, then said he'd be in touch. As we watched him leave, I asked JR, "Now what?"

"I was on the phone with my aunt. She found out about Nick, and she's at wits' end. I tried assuring her it was a mistake. I have to go see her, Hank. Can you drop me off?"

"Of course, I'll come inside with you."

"No, I need to do this alone."

I nodded. "I understand."

JR said, "Hank, I'm going to stay in Florida a while, and as much as I'd like to see you, there's no reason for you to stay. We'll settle up on fees, and my aunt will write you a check."

JR had a glum look on his face like he'd been holding up the world. I knew I couldn't do anything for him, but I wasn't about to leave now. "I'm not going anywhere, and that's final."

He gave me a manly hug. "Thanks."

"You take the car. Nick's building is just up the block. If anything changes, I know how to reach you."

He nodded.

I watched him drive away then started for Nick's building. Like Walker said, finding the killer, if it wasn't Nick, wasn't my problem, and yet, I knew I couldn't let my client down. Walker promised to fill in the spaces, assuming there were any. But that meant finding Elizabeth, and according to Amanda, that might never happen.

I also had another reason to stay: Amanda. I called and asked if she'd mind me sticking around a few days, reminding her it was her idea that we should *hang out.* Or would I complicate matters if her husband returned home?

"Not a problem, Hank. I essentially kicked him out. The divorce papers are in the mail."

I smiled to myself.

"I'll be waiting."

I then called JR and told him where I'd be for a while.

"Lucky you, Hank. I was about to say I'm here if you need me, but that would be foolish. Have fun."

―――――――

After looking around Nick's apartment, I grabbed my carry-on and headed out the door. The CSU had completed its job, including removing Nick's computer from the apartment. The only reminder of a crime was Terry's blood, now dried up.

Under the circumstances, Amanda appeared to be thrilled I'd decided to stay, and when I arrived at her white, single-story house by taxi, she greeted me with a wide smile. Unlike last time at the motel, she was fully clothed in blue jeans and a casual white top.

She reached for me and we shared a lingering kiss. What would the neighbors think? She pulled me inside and shut the door.

"I'm so glad you decided to stay, Hank. I really missed you."

Then after a devilish smile, she said, "I have a little secret: I've only been with two men in my life, you and my husband. By far, you're a much better lover." She giggled. With that, she took my hand, and we started for the bedroom. When we arrived at her bed, she turned, drew me into her, mouth open. We kissed passionately, tearing at each other's clothes, until we stood with little more than smiles, and continued where we'd left off at the motel.

THIRTY

R omance and lust! We didn't leave the house for two days, most of the time spent in the bedroom, except when Amanda slid out of bed—reluctantly—to feed us or replenish our wine glasses. I'd been on a honeymoon years ago with my former wife, Susan. We were young and inexperienced, but we were in love and couldn't get enough of each other.

Amanda had been married once as well, and she, too, recalled the blissful early days of their marriage. And while I had had a few relationships afterward, being with Amanda brought my sex life up a notch. Okay, it was only a few days, but I was smitten. She told me she felt the same. We were in sync in every way, particularly with sex.

After the second night, I was spent. We'd fallen asleep in the late afternoon, and when I awoke, darkness hovered over us. For a moment, I'd forgotten I was in paradise, until the rhythm of Amanda's soft breathing brought me back to reality. I touched her slender arm and smiled. My lover was fast asleep, and as much as I would have liked waking her for another round of lovemaking, water was the answer to my parched mouth.

I crawled out of bed, slipped on my jeans, and tiptoed into the kitchen. Finding the light switch, I turned it on and searched for a glass. Amanda's kitchen was spotless. She either was a neat freak or rarely cooked. I found a glass in one of the cabinets, filled it up from the refrigerator dispenser, and took a much-needed gulp. I could get used to this life of making love and sunshine.

I filled the glass again, crossed the kitchen, and entered the living room. I hadn't been in Amanda's house before and was curious what my new lover's place looked like. I flipped on the light switch and found the room tastefully decorated. She was a minimalist, with two white sofas facing each other, a round coffee table, and an end table on one side of the sofas. What caught my interest, though, was the walnut console table by the window, or rather several five-by-seven picture frames perched on top of it.

As I eased closer, the photos came into view: one of Amanda and Elizabeth, I'm guessing as teenagers, and smiling. A back-yard landscape with trees, plants and lots of flowers.

I picked up the wooden frame. Obviously, better times. Maybe Amanda kept them out of sentimentality. I set it back then selected another photo, this one of a man, handsome, early forties, clean shaven. I assumed it was her soon- to-be ex-husband. I felt a pang of jealousy. But then, Amanda had admitted, I was a better lover.

I chugged down the water and stared at the last photo of Amanda standing next to a woman, around the same age, and smiling in front of a Caribbean resort backdrop.

Upon further observation, I had the strangest feeling. The friend looked familiar, though I was sure we'd never met. I picked up the frame and flipped it over to glimpse the names and dates, but there weren't any. My stare lingered a few moments longer.

"It's a small collection."

I turned and smiled. "But nice."

She walked over and yanked the photo out of my hand. Her eyes fixated on it, followed by a sigh.

"You okay?"

She remained silent, then placed the photo back on the table, her hand shaking slightly. She turned to me with a feigned smile. "Better days."

She recovered, then pointed at the photo of the man. She frowned. "That's going soon. It should have disappeared a long time ago."

"Your husband?"

"I left it for posterity. It'll get burned once the divorce is finalized." Her tone reeked with sarcasm.

"Anyway," I said, "I couldn't sleep, and I was thirsty—"

"You hungry?" she asked with a smile.

"Hungry? Well, I guess I could manage a snack, but it's kinda late for dinner."

She took my hand. "I wasn't thinking food, silly."

After a few days of contentment, I innocently brought up Terry's murder. And while I didn't mention Elizabeth, Nick or Terry by name, Amanda's mood changed from happiness to gloom. Perhaps she wanted to continue in a state of euphoria, forgetting the past, and I got that. Given her acceptance that Elizabeth had vanished, and was probably responsible for Terry's murder, why would she want to engage in a painful conversation surrounding her twin? After all, they were of *one* egg.

Our lovemaking had turned mundane. Amanda went through the motions, the caresses, the kisses, but her deep breaths and primal sounds all but disappeared. I wanted to ask if it was me, but I knew it wasn't. Something had changed on her end.

The next day, at my suggestion, we went to Fort Lauderdale

beach. I hoped the sun and breezy ocean would change her mood, but it hadn't, and we returned to her place a few hours later. I admonished myself for bringing up the murder and sabotaging a potentially enduring relationship.

Damn you, Hank!

Back at her house, we showered, removed the sand from our bodies, and when I attempted to get intimate, Amanda said she was tired from the sun.

She smiled wearily. "Maybe later."

By the end of the day, I realized our budding relationship had fizzled. We'd been sitting for hours, streaming *Homeland,* when Amanda got up and walked into the kitchen. When she returned with a glass of water, her expression turned crestfallen, and I knew I had to leave. I stood and said, "I don't know what's suddenly happened between us, but if it's me—"

"It's me, Hank!" she blurted. "Me." She pressed her lips, placed the glass on a coaster, and offered me a hug. Trembling, she said, "I guess this whole episode with Elizabeth has really got me down. I'm not good at hiding it." She sighed. "I think I need to be alone a while. I hope you understand."

I suppose I did.

She sighed. "I really enjoyed us being together, and I want to continue. But right now, I'm afraid until this...business is over with my sister, I can't make you happy. And I dearly want to." She smiled wistfully, and I returned it.

"Me too."

We stood in awkward silence for a moment, until I asked if I could use her computer to book a flight back home.

"Of course. The computer is on the coffee table. It's not locked, so you won't need a password to get in. In the meantime, I'll whip us up something to eat."

All of a sudden, she sounded upbeat. Strange woman.

I lifted the laptop open, knowing I wasn't about to book a

flight. I just didn't want Amanda to know. When her screensaver appeared, the photo of her and her friend showed up. Screensavers are generally used for decorative or entertainment purposes: personal. What was so personal about their friendship? *Better days* was how Amanda had put it.

I kept studying the face, the smile, and then it clicked: a birthmark on her friend's left cheek. Again, I wondered: where had I seen that face?

"Hey."

My eyes shifted to the kitchen door. "Any luck finding a flight, or am I stuck with you a few more days?" Her laugh was off.

"Not on the site yet."

She crossed the room and looked at the photo, then quickly clicked Google, her hands trembling again.

"I generally use Kayak; they're a good travel site. Let me help." When she arrived at the site, she said, "All yours."

She returned to the kitchen and brought back a mug of coffee that read 'I love me' on it.

"Thought you might want some."

So thoughtful. I am going to miss this.

"Thanks."

She placed the mug on a coaster and glanced at the computer. I had returned to the screensaver and peered up. Her eyes appeared to be burning into the photo.

"I just realized this is the same photo as the one on the table." I peered over at the table, but the photo was gone.

I turned to Amanda. Her eyes remained hard on the screensaver until she slammed the laptop closed. Recovering, she said, "Sorry, you probably didn't book your flight yet." She lifted the computer cover.

That photo. I said, "I was going to, but JR just texted me. Something to do with Nick. His doctor called and told him Nick was making progress and wanted to see me."

She stepped back. "What about?" Her voice fell flat.

I shrugged. "He didn't say, except it had to do with the murder. Either way, I think I'll stay a day longer. I'll go back to Nick's—"

"Nonsense, you'll stay here. As a friend." Another feigned smile. "We'll figure out sleeping arrangements." She then asked, "So, what do you think happened that Nick suddenly came around?"

I shrugged. "I'll find out later. Can you imagine if Nick identifies the *real* killer?"

Amanda sighed. "I think we both know Elizabeth wanted Terry dead…"

Our eyes held for a moment, then as she left for the kitchen, I turned back to the screensaver.

Connect the dots, Hank.

THIRTY-ONE

That night, I hadn't managed to sleep very well. That photo kept nagging at me. Around six a.m., I woke up with a start. I turned to Amanda—her king-size bed kept us safely apart—but she wasn't there. As I took a breath, the smell of coffee wafted over my senses. Good, she was in the kitchen. I stepped into the bathroom and texted JR. I did need him, after all.

Call me at six-thirty.

A few minutes later, he texted back, I was asleep. You OK?

Later, I typed back.

I hopped in the shower, got dressed, and met Amanda in the kitchen.

"Morning," I said. "The coffee smells great."

She was dressed casually in shorts and a T-shirt that read, 'Women do it better.' I was about to ask her 'do what better,' but figured we'd miss the sexy joke.

"I hope I didn't wake you. I couldn't sleep, so I thought I'd make us some coffee. I can make breakfast."

I gave her a friendly kiss on the cheek and filled my cup with coffee. A sip later, I said, "This is all I need, thanks."

She smiled sadly. "Sorry about a missed opportunity last night. I don't know what's wrong with me, Hank. I mean, I do know. It's complicated."

I smiled warmly. "I understand."

My cell phone chirped. "Who the heck?" I looked at the phone. "I have to take this." I got up and stopped at the kitchen door.

"JR, you're up early. What's up?"

My detective buddy was obviously confused, but he assumed I was into something devious and said, "Okay, I'll play along."

I said, "Doctor Powers told you this? That's great." I turned and gave Amanda a thumbs up.

She feigned a smile and walked over to the coffee maker. As I watched her pour a cup, I noticed another twitch from her hand.

"And you're sure of this?" I smiled at Amanda. "Nick wants to see me, *now*? Great. Can you pick me up at Amanda's house?"

JR played along. "You're tired of getting laid, I get it. When and where?"

I held my hand over the phone and said, "Amanda, JR's picking me up. I'll call later when I find out more on Nick."

She nodded. "Right, sure."

I gave JR the address. "Call me when you arrive."

After saying our goodbyes and wishing each other well, I hopped in the car.

"You wanna tell me what that was all about? I thought I was in the twilight zone."

"In a minute. Drive down the block and park."

"Yes, Miss Daisy." He laughed guardedly.

I pointed to a spot. "Squeeze in there."

"Christ, Hank, what the hell is going on?" He parked and turned to me. "Now what?"

"Lower the windows. We might be here a while."

He depressed both sides and turned off the engine. "Next."

I took a breath. "I think there's something odd going on between Elizabeth and Amanda."

"Like what?"

"I don't know, but I need to go back to Nick's apartment and search through his patients' files. I'm interested in the woman who killed herself." I took a breath. "Back at Amanda's house, I noticed a few photos on a table, and one of them was Amanda and a friend who looked eerily familiar."

"Sounds innocent enough."

"I thought so, until I studied the photo. There was something familiar about the friend. I knew I'd never met her, but I was sure I'd seen her. If that makes sense."

Before JR could answer, I said, "When I opened Amanda's laptop, the same photo came up on the screensaver. What's so special about the photo?"

"You mean the relationship."

"Right. That's when things turned weird. When I innocently asked her about the photo, her mood changed, and not for the better. Things went downhill from there until I decided to leave. And get this. When I glanced over at the table later, the photo was missing."

"Sounds like you hit a nerve. And you think you saw the woman in the photo somewhere else. You mean, at a bar?"

I shook my head. "When I had the chance, I began browsing through Nick's patient files. Okay, it wasn't legal, but I was curious about the woman who killed herself. You know me, I'm always searching for angles. That's when I noticed a photo related to a local newspaper obit. The article was sad, as you would expect. But it was the photo of the deceased that caught my eye. She was young and quite beautiful. What caught my attention was the birthmark on her left cheek. Small, yet notice-able. It reminded me of Marilyn Monroe's mole. Sexy. Only sad sexy. I think it's the same woman in Amanda's photo and screensaver."

JR remained silent, but I could tell he was processing what I'd told him. Finally, he said, "Interesting connection."

I said, "What do you make of it?"

He shrugged. "Either a coincidence or—"

"Something sinister," I finished. "That's why I need to go back to Nick's patient file. What if the deceased is the same woman in Amanda's photo?" I stared out the window and watched a jogger pass by. "She would have known Nick was her therapist." I let that stay in the air a moment. "Could it have been planned, that Elizabeth purposely met Nick? And the twins got rid of two *evil* men together?"

"Jesus, Hank, do you know what you're suggesting?"

"A conspiracy."

We waited about ten minutes, and then I called Amanda. She picked up immediately.

"Hank, is everything okay? You left in such a hurry. Is Nick okay?" She kept rambling.

"Great news. I just got off the phone with Doctor Powers. Nick has made stunning progress. Apparently, he's remembering things that occurred over the past week." I glanced over at JR, whose eyes were rolling.

"That's...wonderful. So, he's talking?"

"He's starting to. The doctor mentioned something about a

dissociative fugue—some medical mumble jumble—a temporary state of amnesia that's been reversed."

When she didn't answer, I said, "Amanda, I'm on my way to the hospital now. I'll call when I get more news."

"That would be...great. Yes, please call."

"Can you imagine if Nick can identify Terry's real killer?" I pushed. "I hate to say it, but all roads lead to Elizabeth. She brought him home from the hospital. She must have called Terry and—"

"God, Hank, when you put it like that, it seems so real. That's horrible."

I nodded to JR. "And get this, the police discovered a security camera aimed down at Nick's street. They might be able to home in on the plate number of the car the runner jumped into. The driver's an accessory to the crime. If they find him, he may talk."

"Crazy."

"I know. I gotta run. Talk soon."

I dropped the call before Amanda could reply, then turned to JR, who had a wide smile on his face. "Good work, Detective. Now what?"

I pulled the rearview mirror in my direction. "We wait."

Within minutes, Amanda's red Mustang sped down the street, passing them, and barely stopping at the stop sign.

"That's her."

JR zipped out of the spot and rushed to the stop sign. As he turned, I watched Amanda speed ahead.

"She's certainly in a rush."

"I guess I set her off." I kept my eyes glued to the back of her car. She made several turns before working her way to the interstate. "This might get tricky with all the lanes."

"Hank, you forget, I drive in New York City." He chuckled. "Damn, she's weaving like crazy. She might get pulled over."

"Let's hope not. She's on the phone, and her hands and head are gesturing like crazy. Like maybe she's not too happy."

"I wonder who she's talking to," JR said. "Maybe her partner in crime."

I side-glanced JR. "We'll find out soon enough." My eyes turned back to the road. "She cut someone off and slid into the right lane." I looked up at the approaching exit.

"Damn."

"You know something I don't?"

"She's gonna get off at Marina Mile Blvd. Trust me."

JR entered the right lane and stayed a few lengths back. "I'll be damned."

I smiled. "I know where she's heading. There's an observation area near the airport."

"I'm assuming you've been here before."

"Once, looking for Elizabeth. One of her hiding places from Terry. He nearly caught her."

Amanda took the off-ramp and slowed as she entered the narrow road. "You can leave me off at the Naval Air Station museum up ahead." I pointed. "It's close enough to the parking observation area, and I can move easily between the trees and bushes." JR pulled over, and I was about to get out when a car roared past us. A white BMW. I memorized the plate number and repeated it twice before jotting it down on my phone.

"Could be the same car that picked Elizabeth up at the beach, the one Mrs. Burke might have noticed a woman hop into outside Nick's building." I shifted to JR. "I'm guessing they'll head in different directions on the way out, so you should follow the BMW."

"What about you?"

"I'll be fine. In the meantime, find the owner of that vehicle. I'm texting over the number now."

When it pinged, he said, "Got it."

I jumped out, dashed across the road, and ducked into the woods. I charged onto the trail leading to the parking lot, about twenty feet away. When I reached the opening, I counted five cars, all but two facing the runway, so it was easy to distinguish the two I was interested in. Their windows were open, but only Amanda was visible and talking a mile a minute. I snuck around to get a better peek at the BMW's driver, wondering if it was Elizabeth.

But it was a man. The rear windows were rolled up, so I assumed only the driver was in the car. I snapped a few pictures of the guy with my phone. Was he another member of Terry's posse? And why was he here meeting with Amanda?

A few minutes later, my cell chirped.

"The guy's name is James Nash, and he's from Miller Falls, New York. I think that's the same town as the victim. He goes by Blade, and he's got a record, but no open warrants. Seems he likes to play with knives, hence his nickname. Apparently, he killed someone in self-defense and got off. Be careful, Hank."

"I intend to. So far, they're just talking. I don't see Elizabeth in the car."

"Unless the driver is doing the talking for both of them."

"The tinted windows are too dark to tell. Maybe when he leaves, I'll find a shadow. I'll call you when they head out."

I waited another five minutes, thinking the driver must have been the same guy who picked up Elizabeth at the beach and took her to the hospital. They then drove back to Nick's place where Terry was murdered.

Then what was Amanda doing here?

Amanda turned toward the woods, toward me, and I froze. But her gaze wandered back to the driver. She reached down and brought up something covered by a cloth and handed it to Blade. It was quick, but I swore it was shaped like a pistol. Or was it my imagination?

Amanda rolled up her window and turned to leave. Blade followed, and I called JR.

"I don't have time to get back to you before they leave. Follow the BMW. I'll call Walker. If Blade has a gun, he'll be interested. One thing, JR: don't let the bastard get away."

"What about you?"

"Don't worry; I can grab an Uber."

"Okay, they're heading my way. I better duck before Amanda sees me," he said, his voice rushing.

I called Walker and told him about the exchange. "JR is following the guy now." I rattled off JR's cell number. "Call him."

"Hank, you're not supposed to be involved—"

"Sorry, there's a call coming in. Talk soon." I disconnected, not wanting to be further chastised.

I waited fifteen minutes for my Uber. The driver offered a bottle of water, which I gladly accepted, and took a much-needed sip, sat back, and watched a Delta jet take off.

The driver, a middle-aged guy who went by Buck, rattled off Nick's address.

"That's it. If there's a change, I'll pay extra."

The driver glanced at his rearview mirror. "No problem."

I called Amanda and got her voicemail. No surprise there. I left a message for her to call me. "I'm with Nick. He's made an amazing recovery."

I looked up at the driver, whose eyes stayed on the road. If he was listening, he didn't show it.

When we reached the interstate, JR called. "They went in different directions. I don't know the area, but Amanda got off at

Broward Boulevard. I'm following Blade. Walker called and should be catching up with me."

"Good, Blade's the one we want for now. I'm interested in whatever's in that cloth." I kept my eyes on my driver. I was certain he was listening to every word. "Now, I'm certain there's more to the story than *one* weapon."

"Walker's calling. I'll call you back."

I glanced out the window. We were approaching the Broward Boulevard exit where JR told me Amanda had gone. I leaned forward. "New destination. Get off at the next exit and head east. Can you program an address while driving?"

"No, it's forbidden. What's the address? I'm familiar with the area."

"Hold on." I looked up Amanda's address and passed it on to the driver.

"Not a problem, sir."

When we arrived at her house, her car wasn't in the driveway.

Where are you, Amanda?

The driver turned to me. "This the place?"

I peered up and nodded. I decided to get out and wait. Worst case scenario, I'd call for another driver.

"We're good." I took out a twenty and handed it to him. "Thanks."

I watched him leave, then headed up the walkway, where there were two gray wicker chairs waiting for me. I plopped down on one and stretched out my legs.

As I waited, a dozen or so cars passed by, three runners, and a woman with a baby stroller, but no Amanda.

Fifteen minutes later and with no Amanda, I called her. I received the same unavailable message. I baited her with, "I think the police broke the case. Can't discuss it right now, but call

ASAP. I'm worried about you. Oh, and I'm sitting on your porch. Another beautiful day in Florida."

I assumed that would get her attention, but still, no Amanda. Ten minutes later, JR called.

"Blade stopped for gas."

"Where?"

"At a Shell station on Federal Highway. Apparently, he needed to take a whizz. Walker and his partner were waiting for him outside, but when he started back to his car, he must have gotten spooked and hightailed it out of there. He was pretty quick."

"He's on the loose?"

"For now. Based on your witnessing the exchange between him and Amanda, Walker was more interested in what he might find in Blade's car."

"Don't keep me hanging, JR."

He laughed. "After determining probable cause—him running and leaving that beautiful BMW obstructing the gas pump, they found a nine-millimeter and five grand in the glove compartment wrapped in—get this—a chamois cloth, you know the kind they use for car washing. Walker's having the car impounded, and then they'll bring the gun in for a ballistics test and run the serial number through NCIC."

"And you caught all this?" I asked eagerly.

"From a distance, but yeah, enough to witness what went down. I'm banking the weapon they found inside Blade's car was the second one used to kill the victim. Walker told me Terry was hit by two different calibers."

"Two?"

"Looks that way. We'll soon find out whether the one Amanda transferred to Blake was the second. We know for sure Terry was shot by his own gun found in Nick's hands at the crime scene."

I thought about the twins' relationship. For sure, Elizabeth was more loving and thoughtful than her sister, maybe feeling guilty that she was forced to ask Amanda for help against Terry.

Amanda went through the motion of accepting her sister's dilemma, even going as far as helping her escape from Terry's web. But there was a history between Amanda and her brother-in-law, and not a friendly one. She hated Terry, and slowly became angry, resentful, and scared. In reality, Amanda became unhinged.

Was it possible the gun Amanda transferred to Blade was the second murder weapon used to kill Terry? *Her* murder weapon? She had the motive, means, and opportunity. But why use two guns?

I shivered at the thought of Amanda's recent comment about Elizabeth missing for the last time.

"JR, I think Amanda might have killed her sister."

I called Amanda one more time, and then hung up before her voicemail kicked in. I opened my Uber app, and within ten minutes, I was on my way to meet JR at the Rustic Motel. My guess was Blade would be staying at the same inn as Terry. That was my hope, anyway.

When I arrived, I found my buddy leaning back in the car's front seat, glancing out the window.

"I wanna check if Blade has a room here," I said, sliding into the passenger seat. "If not, we'll check out Terry's room."

"Sounds easy enough. So, what, we just knock on his door after we find out which one it is?" JR shifted in his seat and gave me a look. "You do know we don't have a warrant to enter the premises. Hell, Hank, I'm out of my jurisdiction, and you're not even on the force anymore."

I smiled devilishly. "Me, no, but you might be able to sweet-talk the manager into letting you see the security footage near his room. I'm interested in whether the sisters paid Blade a visit recently. Like *now*. And if one or both entered the room and haven't left, well, maybe the cleaning crew hasn't cleaned up yet."

"You're crazy."

"I'm desperate. Besides, I just want to talk to them."

"Right, talk."

I glanced over at the motel office. There was a middle-aged guy on the phone. JR watched as I tapped into my photo app and scrolled down until I found Terry's not-so-flattering picture. I sent it off to his cell. I then sent the one of Blade I'd taken near the airport. "Two for one."

When his phone pinged, he viewed the photos. "Nice work."

"Now go inside and be persuasive, Detective."

I watched JR enter the office, show his detective shield, and then the photos. The clerk did a double-take, so I imagined it had to be the one of Terry. JR showed him the second photo and he nodded, then motioned JR to follow him. I smiled. Good job, my friend.

Twenty minutes later, JR returned with a wide smile. "The security tapes showed one of the twins entering a room with Blade two days ago, and it doesn't appear she's left yet. Blade, on the other hand, took off not long after they arrived."

"The timeline sounds about right. Could be Elizabeth took off with Blade from the beach before Terry was killed that after-noon. Did Blade return to his room?"

JR nodded. "According to the security footage, he pulled into the lot a little after 6:00 p.m., alone, and then took off thirty minutes before he met up with Amanda today."

"Leaving Elizabeth behind."

"Right."

I said, "And you're sure it was Elizabeth you saw on the footage?"

"Jesus, Hank, how would I know the difference? I'd be guessing." He looked up at the second level. "We'll find out soon enough."

I followed his stare. "Which room?"

"According to the manager, 217." JR pointed. "For a hundred bucks, the manager said he'd give me a few minutes to get back in the car before calling the room." He checked his watch. "I'm guessing we have a minute or so."

"What's the manager going to say to whoever answers the phone?"

He kept his stare at the room. "The police were returning with a warrant."

"There's only one thing," I said. "We're banking that the twin will answer the phone. In the meantime, why don't you call Walker, tell him you found out where Blade is staying. I'm sure he'll be thrilled."

He was about to call when the door to room 217 flew open and one of the twins bolted, gripping a backpack, and rushed clumsily down the stairwell.

"Which one, Hank?"

I studied her, but couldn't tell by the clothes, hair, or height. I charged after her. "Amanda, Elizabeth, it's Hank."

She glanced my way, dazed, and held onto the railing, struggling to keep moving, bumping into the wall, and when I caught up to her at the end of the building, she screamed.

I put up my hands. "It's me, Hank."

She blinked hard. "Hank, what are you doing here?" Her eyes shot in different directions, then back to me. "Were you followed?"

I still hadn't figured which twin I was talking to. "By whom?"

"Blade." She blinked harder, then collapsed in my arms. JR arrived, and we slid her onto the back seat.

"What the hell was that all about?"

I shrugged. "Looks like she's been drugged. She said something about Blade before she collapsed." I glanced to the back seat. Her eyes were flitting. "Maybe the phone call woke her up. We better take her to the hospital."

"No hospital." She waved tentatively. "Take me to Amanda's house."

Elizabeth.

THIRTY-TWO

I eased her out of the car and helped her to the door. She struggled to remove the key from her bag, then handed it to me.

Inside, I asked, "What happened?"

"The crazy bastard. I thought he was going to kill me."

"Blade?"

"The creep." She gazed over at JR. "Who are you?"

"JR Greco, Nick's cousin. It's why I'm here. How are you feeling…Elizabeth?"

"Okay, but I need to sit. I feel wobbly." She struggled across the room and dropped to the sofa. "Hank, please get me a glass of water. I'm really thirsty." She licked her lips.

I went into the kitchen and took a glass from a cabinet. The place was as I had left it that morning. When I returned with her water, JR was sitting on the other side of the sofa, asking a few soft questions.

"Here you go."

"Thanks." She smiled thinly, and her glassy eyes remained on mine.

"I was worried about you. Where have you been all this time? You took off a few days ago in Blade's car." I wanted to scream at her, but she appeared too fragile.

She took a gulp, then coughed. "That day at the beach, Blade left a message on my voicemail. I didn't recognize the number, so I didn't pick up. When I heard the message, he identified himself and said Amanda was inside his motel room and that she was scared—he wouldn't say why, only that she'd locked herself in the bathroom." She stopped, took a breath, and handed me the glass. "More, please."

When I returned, she said, "Blade was worried and wanted me to help."

"And you didn't think it was a ruse? That maybe Terry set you up?"

Her tired eyes gazed at me, then JR. "I was scared for her. That's all I could think about."

JR asked, "How do you know Blade?"

"He's Terry's friend from the carwash business. We were friendly enough. He must have followed Terry to Florida in his own car."

"The BMW."

A nod.

"And he just happened to be near the beach when he called you. That's quite a coincidence, Elizabeth," JR said snidely.

She glared at him. "You think I'm lying? You don't know what I've been through these whatever days it's been. He drugged me, kept me a prisoner for God's sake."

I said, "JR wasn't suggesting *you* were involved in anything, but you must admit, it looks strange, don't you think?"

"Oh." She sipped some water.

"Why didn't you trust me to go with you? I've been on your side since the beginning."

"It wasn't me. Blade told me to come alone, that you would

try to stop me. Look, I know it sounds weird…like I said, I was afraid for my sister and wasn't thinking clearly."

I side-glanced at JR. "And then Terry was murdered? An eyewitness described a woman that matches your description running out of Nick's apartment house—"

She dropped her glass on the area rug, water spraying about. "Nick? Whoa, what are you saying, that Terry was murdered in Nick's apartment? What happened to Nick?" Her wide eyes shifted from me to JR. "Hank, you don't think I—"

"Christ, Elizabeth, the cops are looking everywhere for you. They arrested Nick for Terry's murder and believe you and Blade were his accomplices."

She squeezed her eyes. "This can't be happening." She turned to us. "Nick was in the hospital. We were there together that morning. Do you really think he could have discharged himself in his condition? And kill someone? Get real. He had to—"

"He had help discharging himself. You?"

"No, no, no, no, no. Wait a second. When was Terry killed?"

"The same afternoon you took off on me."

She held up a hand. "Okay, okay." She got up and trudged across the room, stopping a moment to hold on to a wall, then back to us. "Don't you see, that's when I was in Blade's motel room and drugged up. When I entered the room, Amanda wasn't there. Blade stuck something over my nose, and I passed out."

I turned to JR. He shrugged. Back to Elizabeth. "Are you suggesting Amanda killed Terry? Why would she? You wanted him dead, not her. And why would Blade play a part in the murder? He was Terry's friend." I stopped. "And, as for Nick, he was a perfect patsy for you."

"You are so wrong, Hank. I care for Nick. I would never—"

"I guess we'll have to hear Blade's side once he's arrested."

"Terry raped Amanda! He raped her, okay?"

That stopped me cold. It now made sense. Amanda had a reason to kill Terry.

She nodded. "It didn't take long after I arrived that Amanda blamed me for the rape, saying if I hadn't been with Terry, it would have never happened." Her eyes welled. "I swear, Hank, I didn't know until recently. It makes sense. I always thought it was because we squabbled all the time." Elizabeth closed her eyes, shook her head. "In a drunken rage, he told me what he'd done. We argued, and he hit me. I ran out of the house before he sobered up." She opened her eyes. "And then he followed me here, knowing I'd feel safe with Amanda. He threatened her if she didn't tell him where I was hiding."

"I guess her…past returned," I said.

Elizabeth nodded. "Believe me; she wanted him dead too."

We remained silent a while.

JR finally asked, "Why do you suppose Blade was part of the murder?"

Elizabeth swallowed hard. "He and Amanda were an item once. He was upset when she left New York. I think they were in love. At least, he was crazy about her. Maybe he contacted her while he was here, and she told him about Terry…"

And Amanda told me I was the only man she'd been with besides her husband. Another lie.

"If Amanda wasn't in the motel room when you arrived, where do you think she was?" I asked.

"You'll have to ask her. But I can tell you, if she was part of this—especially me being drugged, I'll never speak to her again. She set me up, Hank."

"And Nick."

She sighed. "Please help us."

That was what I intended—assuming Elizabeth wasn't lying. *But how could I trust either twin?*

THIRTY-THREE

My phone chirped. It was Detective Walker. I listened, gazed at Elizabeth, who looked concerned. I nodded, thanked him, and told him we'd meet him at the stationhouse within the hour.

I closed the phone and said, "Blade is still on the loose, but the gun they found in his glove compartment was registered to him. They're doing ballistic tests now. I told him we'd meet in an hour."

I wanted to keep Elizabeth as far away from Walker as possible until we proved she was innocent. I was pretty sure Amanda wouldn't return home, not after I left positive voice messages concerning Nick. By now, she'd be calling Blade, who'd advise her to get out of Fort Lauderdale, and fast.

I turned to Elizabeth. "Wait here until you hear from me. If you're innocent, you'd be crazy to run." My grim expression caused her to nod.

"Promise. Besides, where else would I go? I don't even have a car."

I wanted to remind her that Uber and taxis were readily

available in this neighborhood. "You have a history of disappearing."

"Okay, okay, I get it."

We left Elizabeth in her thoughts and drove to the Fort Lauderdale Police Department.

"Walker sounded upbeat, so I'm assuming he's going to be in a good mood. He said Terry was hit with two rounds, different calibers."

JR said, "Amanda must have been waiting for him and shot him soon after he arrived. Once down, she must have taken his gun and shot him again, for old time's sake."

"She got her revenge all right. And left Nick holding the bag," I added.

"But why? She knew her sister had fallen in love with him."

I shrugged. "I think it had to do with her friend who killed herself. Nick was her therapist."

"That's extreme, Hank."

I felt a wave of sadness coming on. I'd slept with her. More than that, I really liked Amanda.

When we arrived, Detective Walker had a wide smile on his face. "Nice work, gentlemen." He turned to me. "Remind me to give you an honorary detective badge."

"I already have a few, but one more won't hurt." I smiled.

"Of course, you were a detective once. Sorry if it came off wrong."

"Not at all. I'm glad JR and I were able to help."

"And speaking of help, I'd like to know how you discovered this rendezvous between Blade and this woman, who you haven't identified."

I held off a moment, trying to balance my answer. "Her name is Amanda; she's Elizabeth's identical twin."

He looked at me critically. "You're serious? The woman we've been pursuing. So, what, they're in this together?" Walker had a frown, which meant I'd better come clean.

"As I told you, Nick hired me to find Elizabeth. I met Amanda through that search, and we became...friendly."

His forehead creased. "Go on."

I glanced at JR and then back to Walker. "Amanda helped me find her sister. We just sort of hit it off."

"You mean you've been screwing her."

I bowed, then returned his stare. "She wasn't on my radar. All roads led to her sister, but then Amanda changed, and I began having doubts about her." I shrugged.

Walker turned to JR. "Were you a part of this, too?"

"You mean a threesome, no?"

"Don't make this a joking matter, JR. I gave you information that I thought would help. You guys have been holding back."

"Not true," I blurted. "I gave you Blade. I have no idea where Amanda is, but when I find her—"

"You'll do no such thing! You hear me? I gave you some professional courtesy. If I find out you're holding back more on this investigation, I'll have you charged." He pointed at JR. "And you..." He shook his head.

I was about to respond, but Walker put up a hand. "Don't. Until we find out for certain, Nick Ross is still charged with murder. If he's innocent..." He pointed at us. "It's best that you both leave Fort Lauderdale." His glare remained until we nodded.

———

Outside the stationhouse, I snagged JR's arm. "Walker was very specific about us getting out of Fort Lauderdale."

"Pissed is more like it. So, what, we catch the next flight out?"

I looked back at the building. "Yeah, right." While walking

back to the car, I thought about Amanda and how she'd been so lovey-dovey. Was it real before I started asking questions?

As we entered the car, JR turned to me. "I hate to say it, Hank, but Amanda played you."

He read my mind.

"Sorry, my friend, but you have a pattern of getting involved with…similar women."

I didn't want to admit it, but JR was right. I nodded. "It wasn't until I started asking questions about her friend in the photo. Which means I was good for her until I wasn't."

"Look at it this way: how long do you suppose your relationship would have lasted? Especially, considering you live over a thousand miles away from a quickie."

I sighed. "I'd rather not discuss it."

JR squeezed my shoulder. "Let's figure out our next move."

By 6:00 p.m. in January, Florida days crept into darkness, and when we arrived at Amanda's house, the interior lights were still off. Elizabeth had either fallen asleep or had gone on another disappearing act. I knocked on the door and waited. No answer, so I called out. Still nothing.

I shrugged and punched in her cell number, but it went straight to voice mail. I turned to JR. "I hope I didn't make a mistake leaving her alone."

The door was unlocked, which wasn't a good sign. I turned the knob, entered, and flipped on the foyer's light switch.

"Elizabeth, it's Hank."

Still nothing.

I glanced at JR. "What do you think?"

"She could have fallen asleep. She was pretty wiped out."

I nodded, walked over to the living room, and turned on the

light. The glass was still on the floor where Elizabeth had dropped it, but there was no sign of her.

"I'll check the backyard, Hank."

"Okay, I'll start with the master bedroom." When I arrived and hit the light, I saw the unmade bed, and for a moment, replayed a memory of our lovemaking.

I checked the bedroom closet and found women's clothing hanging in front of me, a mix of sundresses, jeans and tops. My eyes shifted to the right side of the closet. Men's clothes: soft cotton business suits and slacks, and casual shirts.

"JR," I called loud enough for him to hear me.

He walked into the bedroom and stared at the clothes in the closet. "What's up?"

I lifted a light blue suit off the rack. "What do you think?"

"About the suit? Hell, I don't own any. Well, maybe one for weddings and funerals." He touched it. "Nice cotton."

"If you were going through a divorce, wouldn't you take your clothes with you? Unless you were in a hurry." I put the suit back on the rack.

"First of all, I would never get married, so divorce is out of the question. But I get your point. Could be a simple explanation. Maybe the guy hadn't found a new place yet."

I shrugged, not convinced. "Amanda said he was away on business."

"There you go. Sounds like an innocent explanation." He walked over to a chest of drawers and opened one. "Underwear and socks." He turned back to me. "What guy leaves his Jockeys behind?"

"Maybe he's not going anywhere. She could have lied about that too. Her fibs keep piling up."

"Yeah, but how would she explain you to her husband, especially if you were shtupping in their bed?" He shrugged and grinned. "I'm afraid you're gonna have to ask when you find her."

"Right, when I find her."

With both sisters gone and my stomach growling, I realized we hadn't eaten all day.

"You hungry?"

"Jeez, Hank, I thought you'd never ask. I could use some protein, like a ribeye steak with garlic mashed potatoes and some greens on the side."

I closed the closet door and did a Google search on my phone. "There's a Chuck Steak House close by."

"Any good?"

"Pretty good reviews. It claims to be a friendly, family-owned restaurant with quality food and good service. It also says they have an early bird, but it's past six o'clock, so we pay full price. You okay with that?"

"I'm not an early bird guy, so I don't care. As long as the food is good."

After a cursory look around, we hopped in the car, and I put the restaurant's address into the GPS. "It says you'll be savoring your steak in a half-hour." We headed east, then north on US 1, the major north-south thoroughfare. As I pulled into the restaurant's parking lot, my cell went off.

I didn't recognize the number but accepted the call anyway.

"Hello?"

"This is no time for food, friend. You need to go back to Amanda's house and look harder. If you want to get Nick off the hook, you'll need to dig deeper."

"Who is this?" I demanded. The male voice on the other end was friendly but straight-forward.

"Someone who wants to make things right for Nick. We both know he wasn't capable of killing anyone, especially in his condition."

I glanced at JR, who had an inquisitive look on his face. "Then why don't *you* make it right and stop jerking me around. If you know something, go to the police."

A long pause. "Because I trust Hank Reed more."

I fidgeted in my seat and glanced out the windshield. There were about ten cars parked, none with their headlights on. Was he here?

I said, "You seem to know about me and Nick. If he didn't kill Terry—I assume you know Terry was the victim—then who did?" I turned to JR and mouthed. "The hell!"

"I wasn't there, so I can't say. I know that *one* of the twins was responsible." He laughed guardedly. "Though between you and me, I can't tell them apart. Now, skip dinner and drive back to the house. Good luck, PI Reed."

"Wait!"

"Oh, and I called on a burner, so you'll have to wait for me to get back to you. It might be sooner than you think." He disconnected.

I looked up at the lighted restaurant sign. My moist mouth had turned dry.

"Hank, what the hell just happened?"

I shifted into drive. "Sorry, JR, we'll come back for steak later."

THIRTY-FOUR

"I didn't recognize the caller," I said, speeding south on Federal Highway. "Not that I know Blade's voice, or anyone else's connected to Terry, besides Sammy, and it wasn't him. Someone might be jerking us around."

"Yeah, but why?"

I didn't know and wasn't about to take a chance, so I sped up and flew through a yellow light in case I was being followed. After checking the rearview mirror and not finding a car tailing me, my body relaxed.

"The caller knew we were at the restaurant. He knew me and had my phone number." I eased up and stopped at a light, then half-turned to JR. "He claims he's trying to get Nick off the hook, apparently through me. How does he even know I'm involved?"

"Sounds like bullshit."

"Maybe, but why is he leading us back to Amanda's house?"

When the light turned green, I stepped on the gas and we rode the rest of the way in silence. The house was dark when I pulled into the driveway.

"I don't remember turning off the lights when we left."

JR removed his Glock. "Let's see what's going on."

I turned off the engine and got out. The door was still unlocked, and I wondered whether my secret caller had made it convenient for us to enter the house the first time.

"After you, JR."

Weapon in hand, he flipped on the foyer light. We waited a few moments, listening for sound. There wasn't any, so I turned on every light in the house, looking around with each flip. "I don't see anything out of the ordinary. Let's search the place again and see if our friend left a sign. Your choice, JR. Where do you want to start?"

"I'm a bedroom guy." He smiled.

I rolled my eyes. "Okay, I'll be in the living room."

Nothing was out of place, and after a few minutes, I called out, "This is a wild goose chase."

He poked his head out of the bedroom. "Nothing here either. I think the guy was blowing smoke up your ass. Maybe the bastard didn't want us to eat."

I perched on the sofa and glanced around, my eyes stopping at the kitchen, or rather, a door leading...to the garage? I hadn't noticed it before and walked over. When I placed my hand on the knob, my cell called out.

I stopped.

A text message.

You're getting warm.

My eyes shot to the kitchen window. *No shadow, but he's watching us.*

"JR, get in here!"

He arrived in seconds. "You look bewildered."

"I'll explain in a minute." I motioned to his revolver.

"Christ."

I opened the door slowly and pawed the wall in search of the switch. When the room lit up, JR asked, "Whose car is that?"

"Looks like Amanda's husband, Billy's. I drove it once."

"The guy on a business trip?"

I nodded as I studied the position of the car. "Don't people usually pull into the garage front first?"

"I don't know. I don't have a garage."

"Right. I'm going to pop open the trunk. Keep your weapon ready." I opened the driver's side door with a rag I'd found on a work bench and pulled the trunk release.

"Shit!"

THIRTY-FIVE

The body—tiny, like a woman—was curled up, but there was no smell, so if she was dead, she hadn't been for long. I turned her around and realized it was one of the twins. She'd been tethered from behind with black heavy-duty cord and duct tape across her mouth.

Her eyes were opened and blinking, and when I peeled back the tape, she let out a gasp.

"Oh, Christ! What happened?"

"Get me out of here."

JR and I eased her out. I snipped off the cord with a knife I'd found on the bench and freed her arms. She was wobbly at first and hung onto me. We helped her into the living room, and she dropped to the sofa. "How did you find me?"

"Elizabeth?"

"Who else would it be?"

"Tell me what happened?"

Her ashen face looked bewildered. "I need water."

I motioned to JR, and when he returned, I said, "Well?"

She took the glass, downed it, and handed it back to JR. "More."

She settled back, rubbed her eyes. "I don't know. Soon after you left, I heard a sound by the door, and when I went to see what it was, this guy—he was tall and wore one of those full-faced masks, so I couldn't—"

"A he?" I interrupted.

"Had to be. He was built like a guy. He was quick and threatened to kill me if I screamed, which I was too numb to do anyway. He tied me up and demanded I tell him who killed Terry. The guy sounded familiar with a scary voice, but the mask muffled his real one. He looked closely at me, I guess, trying to figure who I was, like maybe he knew I was a twin. I was so frightened I blurted, '*Elizabeth* did it.'"

"You?"

"Yes, but I figured the guy knew Terry was after *me*, not Amanda. I didn't want to blame her even though…I really thought he was going to hurt me." She paused to catch her breath. "He demanded to know if anyone else was involved. I told him Blade." She looked to me for assurance. "He must have believed me, but then said he didn't want me to alert them. I told him I didn't know where they were. He lifted me off the floor and carried me into the garage." She looked toward the kitchen. "After he opened the trunk, I begged him not to put me in there. Instead, he slapped tape across my mouth and told me someone would eventually find me. The bastard."

I got up and paced the room, stopping in front of her. "Who's left?"

"What?"

"Well, you'd know if it was Blade, but that wouldn't make sense since he was involved in Terry's murder."

Elizabeth said, "Sammy?" But then said, "No, he's too short and thin."

"He's also in a county cell," I said.

"Oh, I didn't know."

Of course not.

"Hank, I really don't know who else."

"That makes two of us." I thought of my secret investigator, but that wouldn't make sense; he was helping us. I glanced at JR, who shrugged.

"I thought I was going to die in there. Thank God you guys showed up," she said, sobbing.

She apparently had a guardian angel.

I recalled Amanda telling me Elizabeth was afraid of the water and that, as a child, she cut her ankle, producing a small but evident scar. She said it was the only way to tell them apart.

"Let me see your ankles."

"What?"

"Humor me. Just pull up your jeans."

"I think you're a little weird, Hank. Do you get off on women's…ankles?"

I smiled. "Only yours."

She rolled them up. "Satisfied?"

I leaned down and noticed the scar. It was small but noticeable. "Thank you, Elizabeth."

I scanned the room and said, "Someone's been watching us inside the house."

Elizabeth's eyes darted about. "Hank, you're creeping me out. Who would do that?"

I shook my head. "Don't know, but if it wasn't for *him*, you might have died in the trunk."

Her eyes widened. "Who?"

"Somebody called me and guided us back here. Maybe a friend, though he refused to identify himself. You wouldn't know anyone who would do that, would you, Elizabeth?"

She shook her head. "Nobody." She stopped. "Billy's car is in the garage. You don't suppose he was responsible?"

Billy. I walked over to the photos on the console table and picked up the one of Billy standing alone and smiling. While handsome, he appeared short and thin. Besides, why would he videotape the room, especially if he and Amanda were getting a divorce?

And then it dawned on me. "I'll be right back." I went inside and searched the master bedroom. Maybe Billy had a reason not to trust Amanda. I checked underneath the lamps, behind the twenty-one-inch TV on the chest, and everyplace else not tethered to the wall or night tables. I sighed when I'd discovered nothing incriminating. The last thing I needed was to be filmed in *their* bed.

Relieved, I returned to the living room and noticed JR casually lifting trays, lamps, and knick-knacks.

"Anything?"

He shook his head without looking up. "Not yet." He lifted a picture frame off the console table and looked behind it.

He held it up and glanced over at me. "Interesting."

I walked over to him. "I don't remember seeing this one before." The five-by-seven frame showed Yosemite National Park valley at sunset. I asked Elizabeth if it looked familiar.

She shook her head. "Pretty, but no."

JR turned the frame over and smiled. "It's a nanny cam picture frame. Parents use it to monitor the babysitter or nanny who's watching their kids. It works with a smart phone."

"That's how he knew what was going on with Elizabeth."

"Apparently." He waved at the frame, then turned it around toward the wall. "Nighty night."

I thought a moment. "Our Good Samaritan had access to the house, maybe even had his own key." I walked back to the bedroom, searched for a similar picture frame, and I was relieved when I didn't find one. If Billy wanted to check up on his wife, he would have had one sitting here. Still…

Back inside the living room, I asked Elizabeth about her brother-in-law.

"Billy?" Elizabeth shrugged. "Seems like a nice guy, though Amanda told me they were getting a divorce. She didn't say why, but I think it had to do with infidelity on his part. Just a guess."

My phone beckoned me, and I excused myself. It was Detective Walker. He thought he owed us an update for our good work. He told me Blade gave himself up and swore he had nothing to do with Terry's murder, that he was only the driver.

I stepped outside. "Did he explain how the gun and money found their way into his glove compartment?"

"He said the person who hired him wanted it buried. He claimed he was going to the police, but admitted he was going to keep the money."

"I guess he forgot to mention the gun belonged to him."

Walker laughed. "Blade must have assumed he'd obliterated the serial number by filing it down. I explained it didn't work. He then told us she asked for his firearm, just in case, which he now realizes was a mistake. He swore up and down it wasn't him."

"I guess he didn't realize he was an accessory."

Walker laughed. "Blade must have missed that class. He said it was an honest mistake. When we approached him at the service station, he got scared and he ran off."

"Total bullshit," I offered.

"I agree."

"Blade wanted a deal. He said he'd give up the person who hired him for freedom. That would be sweet."

"You didn't?"

"Of course not. I told him I knew it was one of the twins and that when we found them, they'd talk. He wasn't too happy and said he wanted a reduced sentence that he could live with. I hedged, told him there were other things in the mix." He paused. "Blade swore it was Elizabeth and said that had to be worth something. He also claimed he called the cops after she killed her husband. Just in case Terry was still alive."

I smiled to myself. "He's wrong about Elizabeth. She has an alibi."

"Really? How do you know?"

I explained how we found her at the Rustic Motel. "There's a CCTV showing she hadn't left the room until *after* the murder. I can prove it was her and not Amanda."

Walker held off a moment. "Damn you, Hank, I told you to go home." He stopped. "You're sure about this?"

"Yes."

He appeared to be calculating his response. "Okay, I'll have to verify it. We'll talk afterwards."

"What about Nick? Is he still a suspect?"

"Right, Nick. Blade was in a hurry to get a deal, and he swore your client was a patsy." He lowered his voice. "Between you and me, I didn't think he was responsible, but my partner… well anyway, he now agrees Nick is innocent. So, you can finally fly back home and take JR with you." He laughed cautiously. "Look, I know I've been a hard-ass with you guys, but if you're right about Elizabeth, I won't reprimand you anymore." He chuckled. "I'll call after I watch the surveillance tapes."

"Thanks for calling, Detective. I'll pass the good news to JR and his aunt."

Walker disconnected.

I took a deep breath and went back to the living room where JR and Elizabeth were talking about Nick.

He looked up. "Everything okay?"

I smiled. "Nick's no longer a suspect."

"Oh, my God." Elizabeth jumped up and hugged me. "He's coming home?"

"That I don't know. He's still…fragile. He'll need time."

"Still…"

"So, they caught Blade and Amanda?"

"Just Blade." I looked over at Elizabeth. "Your sister is still out there."

She nodded sadly. "She must have held in her rage toward Terry all these years after the rape until he showed up at her doorstep."

That I got. What I didn't get was her rage toward Nick. Or did I?

THIRTY-SIX

That night Elizabeth, JR, and I celebrated Nick's innocence by indulging in thick juicy ribeyes at Chuck Steak House. It had been a long ordeal, and although Amanda was still on the run, we managed to relax over a bottle of wine with past travails momentarily forgotten.

"I'm going to see him tomorrow," Elizabeth said with a smile.

"That'll cheer him up." I raised a glass to her.

JR agreed and said he was happy for both of them. "And my aunt will be ecstatic knowing Nick is in a promising relationship. And now, with the past behind you, I believe you guys will have a bright future."

I asked if she intended on going back to the carwash business.

She shook her head fiercely. "No way. That place was too toxic. It was my idea to open it, but Terry took control almost immediately and started using the business for illegal purposes."

"Money laundering?" I said.

She stared at her wine glass a moment, then, with a nod, said, "I'm going to sell it and stay in Florida. I have too many bad

220

memories in New York." She paused. "I called a funeral home and made arrangements to have Terry cremated. My final duty as a wife."

I ate a chunk of perfectly cooked medium-rare steak and took a sip of Merlot. I looked over at Elizabeth, who was playing with her food. I guess bringing up Terry dampened her evening.

"You okay?"

She met my gaze and nodded. "I'm nervous about making a new start. There are so many things I need to know about Nick, but I don't want to upset him right now. He told me about the divorce. Do you know if it was amicable?"

My eyes shifted to JR, and he nodded.

I thought a moment. "Nick hadn't actually filed for divorce. His wife died in a car accident before it happened. She was pregnant."

"Oh, God, that's terrible. Why didn't he—"

"It's a sore subject, and I'm sure in time, Nick would have told you."

She bowed her head and said, "I wasn't exactly honest with him either. I told him I was never married and that I'm a nurse. I didn't want to spoil the evening. I would have told him..." She looked over at me. "Afterward." A faint smile.

I touched her hand and smiled. "You'll figure it out."

JR said, "You're his angel, Elizabeth."

She sighed, a smile curving her lips. "I'd like to believe that."

After a satisfying meal, we drove back to Amanda's house in silence and bid Elizabeth goodnight, but not before thoroughly checking the house again. On the way back to Nick's place, JR said, "Now that my cousin is in good hands, I'll be heading back home tomorrow. NYPD needs me more than you do, Hank."

"Never."

The next morning, JR picked up his aunt and escorted her to the hospital. Nick was happy to see them, and happier now that charges against him had been dropped. He had asked about Elizabeth, and JR assured him she would pay him a visit later that day.

JR returned to Nick's apartment around noon, and with excitement, told me the visit had gone well. On the way to the airport, JR said, "Hank, I can't thank you enough for helping my aunt and Nick. She's feeling a whole lot better, and believe it or not, Nick is looking better."

"All's good, except for Amanda," I said with a frown. "I hope the cops catch up to her soon. I'd feel a whole lot better knowing I can head home in peace."

"Hell, if I didn't have a deadline on my case, I'd hang around a few days. Too many murders going on in my absence." He chuckled, and after arriving at the JetBlue terminal, we shook hands and exchanged bear hugs. I watched him disappear inside and sighed.

I exited the terminal roundabout and entered the interstate. Since I didn't have another gig, I decided to stay in Fort Lauderdale a few days to recuperate from the twins' syndrome.

About a half-mile from Nick's building, I called Doctor Powers. He was happy Nick was no longer a suspect but believed he should have stayed a while longer before being discharged.

"I was against it, of course, but he and Elizabeth were convinced, now that the murder was solved, his positive mental health would improve at home."

"You released him?" I asked, knowing what he'd told me.

"Like I said—"

"Yes, I heard you. Okay, I'm heading over to Nick's apartment."

"They seemed happy when they left."

"I'm sure." I hung up, unsettled. Elizabeth had said nothing about Nick being discharged. Picking up speed, I arrived at Nick's building in fifteen minutes. I skipped the elevator for the stairs, and when I arrived at the door, I knocked. "Nick?"

I didn't like that he didn't answer and let myself in.

I took out my phone and called Elizabeth.

"Where are you?" I demanded.

"At Amanda's. Why?"

"Did you visit the hospital yet?"

"No, I was about to leave in a few minutes. What's wrong?"

"Nick checked himself out, apparently with Amanda's help. She obviously pretended to be you, and I have no idea where they went."

"Oh, God, you don't think—"

———

Where was my phantom text guy when I needed him? For a quick moment, I wondered whether his intention had been to get Nick out of the hospital. For what? Revenge?

I called JR, but it rolled over to his voice mail.

"If you're still in town, call me immediately." I called Detective Walker and told him what I'd learned about Amanda and Nick. "She checked him out pretending to be Elizabeth, and I have no idea where she took him."

"Not good. I just viewed the surveillance tapes. If it's true that you picked up Elizabeth at the motel, then it's her sister I'm after."

"Amanda had no reason to help discharge Nick unless she had bad intentions. And he obviously wouldn't have known it was her; he'd just assumed she was Elizabeth."

"And you're sure Elizabeth didn't pick him up at the hospital?"

"I just spoke to her. She's staying at her sister's house. Look, if you want to confirm it, be my guest. The only difference between them is a scar on Elizabeth's left ankle. Make sure she shows you; otherwise, you might be talking to Amanda."

"How the hell would you know that? Never mind, give me the address."

I did. "I'll call Elizabeth and tell her you're on your way."

"Fine." He paused. "I'm afraid to ask where you're going."

I had a place in mind, but held off telling Walker. "Not sure."

He grunted. "I want to know what you're up to at all times. Do you hear me?"

Fingers crossed. "Of course."

"Why don't I believe you?" He disconnected.

The first place that came to mind was Nick's office. I did a quick Google search. If Amanda's warped mind was playing games, she'd start from the beginning: the therapy sessions. I started the engine and pulled out quickly, cutting off a car. After a few turns, I arrived at a two-story office building in less than five minutes.

I ran inside and located the directory. Nick's office was on the first floor, on the other side of the building. Approaching the office, I heard a woman's voice rambling from inside. She sounded angry and accusatory and threatening.

Amanda.

I grabbed the doorknob, but it was locked. I pounded on the door.

"Amanda, it's Hank. I know you're in there. The cops are on their way. It's over."

When she didn't respond, I shouted, "If you hurt him, you'll never see daylight again. Damn it, Amanda, open the door." I pounded until the door opened ajar.

She appeared, partially obstructing my view. Her face was an angry sight, her matted hair a mess. She held a bloody six-inch kitchen knife in her hand. "He killed my best friend, Janice."

I stepped back.

Amanda's eyes were raw with anger. She held up the knife. "Go away, Hank. I don't wanna hurt you."

My sense was Amanda had managed to incapacitate Nick. He was sobbing in the background, but I couldn't see him. I glared at Amanda. "This is madness. You can't believe Nick was responsible for your friend's death."

"Nick?"

My eyes narrowed on her. "Who the hell's in there?"

She shifted the door wide enough for me to see. I looked in, then turned to Amanda. "Who is he?"

She snarled. "My bastard husband, Billy. He was sleeping with her. *He's* responsible for her death."

"You're not making sense."

Her eyes came alive. "I was waiting for him to return from his trip."

I held up a hand. "I get it, Amanda. But killing him won't bring back Janice. You'll go to prison. Please don't do this."

"It's too late, Hank."

"But—"

She turned her wrist, placing the knife in a threatening position, and I stepped back, praying she wouldn't mix me up with Billy.

She sneered and held up the knife. "I got the bastard to admit what he did. It's over for him," she spat. Amanda attempted to shut the door, but I pushed hard and knocked her off-kilter. As I went for the knife, she thrust it at me and nicked my arm.

Her eyes went wide, and she pushed past me, knife in hand, and rushed out the door. I ran inside and found Billy slack on the patient's chair, bleeding profusely from his stomach, his eyes closed.

I glanced at my wound and frowned, then called for help. I ran to the bathroom and grabbed paper towels from the dispenser and placed them against his wound. I tried stanching the flow of blood, but it wouldn't stop. I shook off the blood where I'd been cut and removed the phone in my pocket to call Walker.

When he answered, I filled him in on Billy, then added, "Amanda didn't bring Nick here, and I have no idea what she did with him."

Walker started to say something, but I glanced down at Billy, his lids fluttering, and said, "I gotta go." I disconnected, then told Billy, "The paramedics are on their way. Stay with me."

I sat with him, waiting anxiously, but by the time the medics arrived, he was dead. They bandaged me up, and I told them I'd wait for the police.

After they left, I called Elizabeth and she picked up on the first ring.

"I'm at Nick's office. Your sister just killed Billy."

"Her husband?"

"I guess she couldn't wait for the divorce. Nick isn't here. Where would she have taken him?"

"Oh, God, let me think. Here? No, I can't imagine. I really don't know, but please find them—"

"I intend to. And call me if you hear from her." I hung up.

An idea came to me, but I needed to act quickly before the office became an official crime scene. Nick told me he had a file cabinet at his office and home. I looked around, and when I found it, rummaged through the files until I found what I wanted.

In the distance, the sirens blared. I'd previously gone through Janice Brandt's file at Nick's apartment, but now I was looking for anything I'd missed before. I skipped several pages. I had already read that Janice admitted to Nick that she was sleeping with her best friend's husband. I now knew it was Amanda's husband, Billy. Janice had been vulnerable from a past relationship, and *he* came on to her.

My brain took in as much as possible as the sirens roared in the distance. I wiped sweat from my brow and read faster, hoping for something new.

I stopped, frustrated. Nothing shot out at me, and after a few moments, I flipped to the end of the file where Janice promised Nick she was ready to confess her affair and beg her friend's forgiveness, which he encouraged her to do. I wondered if she told Billy of her intention. If so, he might have tried to stop her. Did he encourage her to take an overdose? Or did he do it himself?

Shivers shot down my spine. But what had Nick done to deserve retribution? The meds? Amanda must have blamed Nick for being Janice's druggist. So where would Amanda be taking Nick for his punishment? I looked at the obituary once more and made a judgment call.

As the cops approached the door, I stuck the file back.

"In here," I called out, shutting the drawer.

A perfect storm by accident? Elizabeth had begun a relationship with Amanda's best friend's therapist. That must have set her off and accelerated her intentions.

A real mental case.

"I'm opening the door," I called out, and when I did, Detective Walker's stiff expression told me I was in deep shit.

"Nice to see you again, Hank."

THIRTY-SEVEN

I rushed through events with Walker and promised to call later. He wasn't happy and pointed to the door.

Amanda would be long gone unless she had a plan, and my concern was that her plan was to kill Nick. Desperate, I went with my gut, and as I pulled out of the parking lot, a text message came in. It was my guardian angel instructing me to drive to the Evergreen Cemetery in Fort Lauderdale. He included the section and gravesite.

My gut was right.

I punched the information into my GPS, and a minute later, I was driving through local streets, and in less than twenty minutes, reached the cemetery. Inside, I worked my way around until I found the section. The cemetery had few visitors, and none of the cars looked like Amanda's. I emerged from the car, and in the distance, saw a man sitting on the grass in front of a headstone, his head bent, as if he was praying.

I looked around and saw a woman heading toward the guy. From my vantage point she looked like Amanda, same shape and hair. I ran and called out Nick's name, forgetting cemetery noise etiquette. The woman turned and frowned. Not Amanda.

Nick's head turned to my voice, and he glanced over his shoulder and smiled.

"Are you okay?" I said, reaching him. At the corner of my eye, I watched the woman kneeling at a gravesite twenty feet away. Sorry about that.

Back to Nick, I looked for signs of a struggle, but he appeared unhurt.

As he nodded, tears streamed down his face. I sat opposite him on the freshly cut grass and waited for him to speak.

He sighed. "I should have visited her before. I'm so sorry, Janice."

My eyes did a quick search around. "How did you get here?"

He squeezed his eyes. "She called herself Amanda, said she was Elizabeth's twin sister. I didn't know she had one. She was very nice and told me she'd come back once she finished her chores."

Finishing chores was an understatement.

"I'm assuming she told you she was Elizabeth when she arrived at the hospital."

He nodded slowly. "She told me the truth when we got here. She said she wanted to visit a friend. I didn't know we were going to see Janice. I asked how she knew her. That's when she told me her real name and told me Janice was her good friend, and she knew I was her therapist." He looked at the gray-bronze headstone and wiped his eyes. "She was so young."

I read over at the dates and nodded. "She was. But it wasn't your fault, Nick. It was Amanda's husband. She was having an affair with him."

"She—Amanda, told me she was angry when Janice took her life. She first blamed me for prescribing antidepressants. I can't prescribe medication because I'm not a psychiatrist, so I referred one to her, but that's not the point. The idea came from me. I swore I didn't know she would take so many at one time. There were no red flags. I then told her Janice intended on telling her about the affair and to ask for forgiveness." He picked up a blade of grass, felt the texture, and tossed it on the ground.

"Did she?" I asked, knowing. "Forgive her?"

Nick pulled another blade of grass from the ground, played with it, and continued. "Janice died before she had a chance. During our last session, she said she needed more time to build up courage. I told her she'd make the decision at the right time." He paused, dropped the strand of grass on the ground.

Nick continued. "When I told Amanda, she cried, and then forgave me. She realized I had Janice's best interests at heart. But then she became upset and told me she had to leave but would return."

"She's not coming back, Nick. Not today, not ever."

"Oh." His expression turned to confusion. "How did you know I was here?"

I smiled. "You have a guardian angel."

I called Elizabeth and told her to meet us at Nick's apartment. She arrived first and waved as we pulled up. Nick smiled and waved back. I spent an hour with them, making sure Nick was okay. He had made progress over the past few days, and ironically, I believed his meeting with Amanda had helped.

I took Elizabeth aside and asked how Detective Walker's visit had turned out.

"He wanted to see my scar, just like you." She chuckled. "I guess the fall years ago helped."

Indeed, it had. "And that you were no longer a suspect."

She nodded. "He told me he viewed the security tapes, and

based on your statement, accepted my alibi." She sighed hard. "Thank you, Hank, for getting me out of this mess." She sighed again. "But how will I ever deal with Amanda's actions?"

"You will in time," I assured. "Right now, you and Nick need to work out your future together."

She nodded, glanced into the next room. "I'd like to get to know him a lot more. From there, who knows? He needs to get better, and I want to help with that too."

I told her the police might call or pay her a visit every now and then until they found Amanda. "Be truthful."

She nodded. "Promise. This is my chance," she said, then laughed softly.

I looked inside. "Take care of Nick."

I walked into the next room and sat beside him. "I think you and Elizabeth have something real."

He nodded. "It's been a crazy time for me, but I'm a positive guy. I feel a little stronger than yesterday, and hopefully stronger tomorrow. Thanks for finding her." He smiled. "She wasn't made up, Hank. I'm glad you see that now." He shook my hand. "Best to JR."

I stood outside Nick's building feeling hopeful life would work out for the couple. My Uber driver arrived in ten minutes, and I hopped in the back seat.

The driver turned to me. "You requested Fort Lauderdale Beach, right?"

I smiled. "Where else would I go in January?"

Last-minute hotel rooms were scarce, but for an exorbitant price, I found one directly across from the beach. I purchased a bathing suit from the hotel's gift shop, and in ten minutes, I was breathing in moist, briny air. I found a bar on the corner and ordered a much-needed drink. The bartender returned with my beer, and I took a slug. Then another. I checked the beach area. I could get used to South Florida.

Finishing my brew, I strolled along the beach, mulling still unfinished business: the text guy. If only I knew who he was. But some things in life can't be solved.

A half-hour into wading in the water, my cell chirped. The glare from the sun blocked the incoming text, so I shielded the phone.

It's not over, friend.

Now? Damn, I was just getting used to this. When he didn't continue, I punched in, What's not over?

Amanda.

Who the hell are you??

A friend, came back.

I searched the beach area and thought of Robert DeNiro in *Taxi Driver.*

You looking at me?!!!!

LOL. I loved that movie.

Yeah, well go to the police. I'm sunning.

This is personal.

Personal.

I typed, How personal?

A past made right.

Christ.

Trust me. You'll have to leave the sun tomorrow.

My friend hadn't sent me on a wild goose chase before, so I was mildly interested. Actually, I was intrigued.

I'll be waiting, I typed back.

Our communication ended, and I headed back to the bar and ordered a double scotch—neat.

My sleep was erratic, and I woke several times, wondering where my new text friend was sending me. I was up by six a.m. and made a strong cup of coffee in my hotel room.

Text already!

At eight, I went in search of breakfast, finding Rick's Simply Great Coffee cafe a few blocks from my hotel. I selected a quiet booth in the corner, and when the server arrived, a young brunette with a charming smile, and asked for my order, I made it simple: two eggs over medium, rye toast, and lots of coffee.

While waiting for my food, I called Elizabeth. After several rings, she answered with a friendly, "Morning, Hank."

"I guess my caller ID gave me away."

"It did," she whispered. "And I know why you're calling. You're gonna ask if everything is okay, right?"

"You got me." A soft laugh.

"We're in bed. Nick's still sleeping."

"Sorry to disturb you."

"You're not. It's nice knowing you care." She giggled softly. "And I promise not to open the door to strangers."

"Or Amanda."

Her laugh crackled with tension. "Especially her."

By nine, I finished breakfast and strolled across the street to the beach. As I passed bikini-clad bathers, my phone buzzed. It wasn't my phantom friend; it was JR.

"Hank, sorry for the delay. My voicemail was swamped. What happened?"

I told him about the previous day. "Jesus," he said, "bad timing. Sorry I wasn't around for the fireworks."

"Just as well, it wasn't pretty. But the good news is Nick and Elizabeth are safe, so no worries. I did the panicking yesterday." I paused. "I've been waiting for the text guy to contact me. He's got me on another mission, something about Amanda. I'm not sure I want any more excitement with her."

"You trust him?"

"The guy's been right so far. I'm just getting antsy."

"What the hell does he know that the cops don't?"

"Beats me." I heard a text coming through. "Gotta run."

He apologized for the delay. Then added,

It will be worth it.

I found a bench near the lifeguard shack and sat.

Talk to me, I punched in.

He sent me a long-linked message. At first, I thought he was crazy, but it finally made sense.

You're sure about this????

I am now.

I need to make flight arrangements.

No rush, friend. You have a Chance.

My eyes held onto the last word. Was he sending a cryptic message by capitalizing the C in Chance? Was he finally identifying himself? Wasn't he supposed to be dead?

I called JR.

"I need your help."

"Anything."

"Your aunt told you Nick's fishing buddy, Chance, was dead, right? What if he isn't dead? What if Chance is my text buddy? The last message I received a few minutes ago said, 'you have a Chance' with a capital C. Coincidence?"

"Maybe he was in a rush and…forget that. Okay, you want me to find out if he's dead?"

"I do. Why would he be hiding behind a text and being evasive? Something's off, JR. Press your aunt to give you his full name. And if she doesn't, ask Nick. She might be holding back."

"I'll check."

"Come to think of it, why would he bother finding Amanda? Nick is free," I said. "And how the hell is he able to get this information unless—"

"Maybe he's law enforcement. If he is, he'll bring Amanda to justice."

"Through you," he added.

We disconnected, and I returned to the hotel, jumped on the guest computer, and made flight reservations.

I had only told JR my plans, and by six-thirty that evening, after checking in my carry-on carrying my locked sidearm, I was on an Allegiant flight to Syracuse, New York. Once there, I had an hour's drive to Miller Falls, arriving around midnight. I picked the Budget Inn in the heart of the downtown area.

When I arrived, I texted my *friend*, telling him I was safe and sound.

Wanna meet for a drink? I asked seriously.

An early rise. Text you at eight.

Like I was about to sleep. I tried, and eventually nodded off around three, after a quick bathroom run.

My cell alarm greeted me at seven. After showering and making a cup of coffee, I sat and waited. He was prompt.

Ready?

I punched in a thumbs up.

ET's Carwash. Good luck.

ET, Elizabeth and Terry's carwash. I arrived in five minutes and found a dozen cars lined up. I was told snow had blasted through the area five days before, and drivers were lined up to rinse salt off their cars. My rental didn't need washing, so I parked just outside the business property and got in line.

After a customer received a ticket, they entered a long interior walkway toward the cashier. Along the way, customers were treated to watching each stage of the washer/dryer operation, which ended at the cashier's booth.

I stood behind a guy wearing a Mad Bomber hat. When it was my turn to get a ticket, I pointed. "I'm with him."

The Mad Bomber guy, around sixty, seemed to enjoy the show. He was on the phone with someone describing every detail. What else was there to do in winter in Miller Falls?

The guy was getting on my nerves. I mean, he kept pointing to an old, shitty blue Ford Fiesta, for God's sake. Turn it in already!

Slow down, Hank.

My heart raced. Would Amanda be standing behind the plexiglass window collecting the payment with a smile? And if so, then what? I couldn't arrest her. All I could do was threaten.

Stepping closer, three people in front of me, I tucked my hands in a coat I'd brought from home to Fort Lauderdale. The cold was especially intense, or was it my fear of what I'd find?

Two people left. I looked around. Outside of the sounds from the machines soaping, rinsing, and drying, it felt eerily quiet. Approaching, I wondered what Amanda was doing here in the first place. She wasn't the owner, and as far as I knew, Elizabeth hadn't handed over the keys to the business.

Or had she?

But what the hell did Amanda know about the carwash business?

The Mad Bomber hatter in front of me turned to pay, pushing his receipt and a ten-dollar bill through the narrow plexiglass slot. He had a dour expression and remained silent.

My turn. I took a deep breath, walked up to the booth, and made eye contact with the cashier. It wasn't Amanda; it was Terry's sidekick, Sammy. What the hell was he doing here?

He smiled. "Where's your ticket?" he asked politely. He obviously didn't recognize me, and I suspected it had to do with the black wool cap pulled down above my eyes.

"You have a ticket?" he asked again.

"Sorry, I lost it."

He frowned. "Seriously? Well, I gotta charge you for the works then. Ten dollars."

I took out a ten, handed it through the slot, and said, "I thought you were sitting in jail." I removed my cap and smiled.

His eyes widened. "The fuck."

"Amanda pay your bail?"

At first, I thought he was going to dive through the plexiglass, which made no sense considering it was smaller than a medicine cabinet. He stopped, realizing it wasn't a good idea, and high-tailed it to the back.

"Amanda!" he yelled.

She was here. I looked around for an entrance, and when I found it, raced inside. Sammy charged out, glaring at me, and holding a black pipe in his hand.

"You fuck."

He swung high, and I took a glancing blow to the shoulder. I dove into him, knocking him against a wall, but he held onto the pipe and tried to thrust it at me. I grabbed his wrist and twisted it, the pipe dropping to the floor. Sammy yelped in pain.

"What's going on?" a customer cried out.

"Call the cops," I demanded.

Sammy headbutted me and shot his hand downward toward his ankle. I kicked him in the groin, and he wailed as I jammed my fist into his solar plexus, and he dropped.

"Where is she?" I demanded, jerking him off the floor.

He was dazed and moaned. I turned my head and heard a commotion coming from outside. I pulled Sammy's knife out from his ankle sheath and pocketed it. Someone was yelling that his car was being hijacked. I dropped Sammy to the floor and ran out.

"She took my car!" an elderly guy cried. "I just bought it."

I ran up to him. "What make was it?"

"A white Camry."

"A woman?"

"I think the owner. What the hell!"

Right, what the hell!

Amanda made a quick right onto a main road. I ran to my rental and struggled to insert the key in the ignition. I finally engaged the engine and shot out, but a slow-moving sanitation truck spreading salt blocked my view of the road.

Reaching the light, I took the same right turn as Amanda. The traffic was slow, but she was weaving in and out between cars. I flashed the cars in front of me to move aside and caught up within a hundred feet from her when the light up ahead turned yellow. She sailed through it, and I followed, nearly clipping a pick-up truck.

I speed-dialed JR, and when he answered, my voice rushed. "I'm chasing Amanda in Miller Falls. You need to call the locals."

"Can you be more precise, Hank?"

"Hold on." I drove another fifty yards before catching a sign. "I'm on Holly Road heading, hell, I don't know, but I just passed a Walmart on my right. Can't be too many of them locally." I disconnected, dropped the phone on the passenger seat, and upped my speed. I was gaining, but she took a hard right down a narrow two-lane road. I stepped on the gas, but she was driving crazy. My speedometer was north of sixty in a thirty-five-an-hour zone. The snow hadn't melted, and her car began to swerve.

This was madness, but Amanda wouldn't stop.

Until she did.

Fifty yards ahead, she slammed head-on into a chestnut oak tree. I skidded up over the curb and was able to stop before plowing into a light pole. I jumped out of my car and raced to hers, but the driver's side door was open, and when I peered inside, she was gone.

She had managed to unbuckle her seatbelt and take off. I glanced at a nearby, sparse-winter woods and noticed a trail of blood. I spotted her stumbling past a giant oak.

"It's over," I called out. "The police are on their way."

She staggered and tried to bore on, then wobbled at a crawl. Leaning onto a tree, she turned to me, her face bloodied and one arm hanging limp.

At first, I had my doubts. Maybe it was the blonde wig, but her soft smile told me it was Amanda.

"It's over," I repeated, catching up to her.

"How?" she forced.

"Find you? I have a friend. He told me you'd be here."

"Friend?"

"Long story, but yeah." I looked over my shoulder, then back to Amanda. "You'll be arrested for the murders of Billy and Terry. As for Billy, it would have been easier to divorce him."

Amanda's glossy eyes settled on mine.

"Janice was vulnerable," she struggled, "and he took advantage of her. She realized being with him was wrong. Nick told me she was about to confess." She stopped, caught her breath. "I got Billy to admit he persuaded her to take an overdose of pills, the bastard. He killed her, Hank. And he paid for it."

I let her have her say and nodded. "How come you didn't kill Nick when you had the chance? You blamed him—"

She waved her good arm. "I forgave him—"

"Yet you set him up after you murdered Terry."

She winced in pain. "I was angry. I thought he could have done more to help her." Her chest heaved and her breathing faltered. "I realized after talking to him at the cemetery that I was wrong."

Sirens echoed in the distance. I asked Amanda if she had anything else to tell me before they patched her up and took her away.

She coughed, blood oozing from her mouth. She touched my arm for support. Or maybe more. "I wish things had been different between us. I think we fit well together." She kissed my cheek.

A police car pulled up next to the wreck.

"Where are the paramedics?" I called out.

The patrolman's eyes shot up toward us. "They're on their way," he shouted, walking toward us.

I sensed Amanda was in a great deal of pain and pleaded, "Don't give up on me. They'll be here any minute."

She placed her head in the crook of my neck and with labor, whispered, "I could have loved you more."

I smiled softly and nodded. "Me too."

"Please tell Elizabeth I forgive her."

I held her, gave her a final kiss, before she went limp in my arms.

THIRTY-EIGHT

As the ambulance barreled away with Amanda inside, I returned to the white Camry she had stolen, now embedded in the tree. The young uniformed patrolman, who identified himself as McCabe, began firing off questions, and I answered a few, including identifying the crash victim.

At the corner of my eye, I noticed a car parked haphazardly across the street. A curious motorist?

"Be right back." I hustled toward it, but as I stepped within recognition of the driver, the black Hyundai shot out and sped down the road too fast to get a plate number. I had a sense it was my text friend in a rental.

Upon returning, Mc Cabe asked, "You know the guy in that car?"

"Guy?"

"Well, whoever?"

"No. Must have been a curious bystander," I lied with a shrug.

"I knew her sister," McCabe started. "Through the carwash business. Nice lady. Didn't know she was a twin." He stopped and frowned. "Didn't think too much of her husband. I knew he was shady, and some say he had connections with local cops, so they left him alone."

"I heard that too."

"Rumor had it she ran away from the creep. Marital problems. She ever divorce him?"

"Too late for that. He was killed in Fort Lauderdale by her sister." I nodded toward the Camry.

"No shit." He thought a moment. "Let me get this straight. Amanda killed Elizabeth's husband, and then she comes here pretending to be…Elizabeth. So, you think they cut a deal? You kill my husband and earn a carwash business?"

I smiled. McCabe had a point. "We'll have to find out." I asked him if he knew a guy who went by Blade.

"Oh yeah. Didn't care for him either. He was part of Terry's circle. He involved in the murder, too?"

I shrugged. "Looks that way. He's sitting in a Broward County jail cell."

After a few moments, McCabe sighed. "Anyway, I'm gonna need you to come back to the station and fill out some forms."

"I'll follow you."

I was a few miles out of town when my cell pinged.

Good job.

I don't usually text and drive, but I responded with, Thanks Chance. Why did you drive away?

Wasn't me. Safe trip home.

Was it a coincidence an uninterested party stopped near the crash site?

So, you don't want to meet for a beer? I asked.

LOL

Inside the station, I answered a bunch of questions, and McCabe and I exchanged business cards. I added Walker's name and number to the mix.

"I'm sure he'd appreciate any update on Amanda."

He nodded.

"I'm staying at the Budget Inn, but only until tomorrow morning, so if you need me for anything, give me a shout."

Heading back to the inn, I stopped across the street from the carwash. A few people mingled about, including employees, probably waiting for the boss to return. I didn't have the heart to tell them she was in the hospital, dead or alive.

Sammy wasn't among them, so I figured he'd split. My guess was Amanda bailed him out to help with the carwash business. He ran it with Terry.

The guy whose car Amanda swiped was still around. I hated to break the news to him. He'd be smart to call a taxi.

Back at the Inn, I called JR and Detective Walker in that order. JR was ecstatic.

"We gotta send your text guy flowers." He laughed. "Now that we know he's not dead. Chance, whose real name is Sean Abbott, recovered from, get this, the car accident involving Nick's wife. He was her lover. My aunt finally admitted that Chance was dead to the family for obvious reasons. I guess now he's trying to do right by Nick."

"I'll be."

"What can I say, the whole thing was a tragedy. Including Amanda."

I sighed. "For sure."

We disconnected and I called Walker. He was flummoxed that I found Amanda in New York, no less.

"I'm gonna hold off asking how you managed that one, Hank. But thanks. Are you returning to Fort Lauderdale, because beers are on me?" He laughed, then mumbled. "You're a hard one to figure out, Reed."

I wanted to call Elizabeth, but until I found out her sister's condition, I held off.

I needed to see Amanda, maybe for the last time, and called

McCabe. He arranged to meet me at the Miller Falls Hospital in a half-hour.

With his help, I was allowed into her room, where she was hooked up with tubes, her eyes closed. While McCabe stood by the door, I lingered about ten minutes, saying a prayer and thinking about our short time together. When her doctor arrived, he sounded pessimistic about her prognosis. I handed him my card. "She's wanted for murder."

His eyes widened. "So, the crash wasn't an accident?"

I glanced over at McCabe. "It was, except she was running away from justice." I sighed. "Apparently, she reached her limit."

The doctor glanced over at Amanda, then checked my card. "You're working with the police?"

I nodded. "I also know the patient. If you would call the patrolman here with any updates, I'd appreciate it."

He looked over to Amanda and nodded.

On my way out, I gazed over at her one more time and sighed.

At one o'clock, I returned to my room to collect myself. Having the weight of the past events on my mind, I pulled up a chair facing the window overlooking the downtown area. It was a cold and dreary day, kind of like my mood. So much tragedy had happened, but I tried focusing on Amanda and our short but sweet time together.

Would I ever see her alive again? And while her future was bleak if she lived, I couldn't help but wish the past few days never existed. My thoughts kept returning to her final loving words: "I could have loved you more."

I think I could have too.

After booking a flight back to Fort Lauderdale for the following day, I texted Chance.

I was told you were dead. R U Lazarus?

I waited and thought I'd chased him away, but a few minutes later, he wrote.

I screwed up and lost a close friend. Was dead to him. Trying to make things right.

He didn't say *how* he screwed up, but I knew. I asked whether he'd like to get together for a drink and discuss the screw-up part.

Have a nice life.

Amanda didn't make it. The doctor called around seven that evening. "Complications" was all he said.

The 'what ifs'? turned to reality, and I felt only sadness. For both of us. I held off calling Elizabeth, instead punching in Walker's number. I told him he no longer had a suspect and asked if he would pay Elizabeth a visit since I wasn't in a talkative mood, nor did I want to break the news by phone.

That night, after a few drinks, I struggled to sleep. So, what was new? Late the following morning, I was on a flight back to Fort Lauderdale. Walker would certainly want to talk, and I needed to see Elizabeth and Nick.

With my phone in airplane mode, I missed a text message, which I picked up upon arrival.

The message read,

We have a problem. Terry has a brother. Rick. Could be looking for vengeance.

Back to him, Sorry just arrived at airport. Might have to contact police.

He hasn't done anything yet.

Chance was right. Unless Rick threatened them, the police wouldn't get involved.

What's the plan?

I'm on it. Stay tuned.

Stay tuned?

I called Nick, but it went straight to voice mail. The same for Elizabeth. Maybe they were frolicking or…I grabbed a taxi outside the terminal building, and once inside, called them again. No luck.

The driver stopped in front of Nick's building. All quiet.

Instead of ringing his bell, I used the spare key I'd kept and double-timed up the stairs. When I reached his floor, I caught my breath and approached the door. I was about to insert the key when I was startled by a gunshot, followed by a scream.

I called 911, then removed my revolver and inserted the key. Arms extended, my hands slippery with sweat, I squatted and pushed the door forward.

A man lay on the floor, face-up ten feet from me, blood seeping from a chest wound.

"Police," I shouted, my eyes swinging toward the bedroom.

I heard a thump, as though someone had landed on the floor. I crept toward the bedroom. I needed to know where they were positioned and yelled, "I killed your brother, Rick. The bastard had it coming."

Three shots splintered the wall above my head.

I dropped to the floor, then took a breath.

"Good try. Be a man and come out. Not like your brother."

Another two shots. Inches away.

I swallowed hard then called out. "You okay, Elizabeth?"

A muffled response. I pictured Nick's bed. Her voice came from the left side.

"Where's Nick?"

"He's in here, whoever you are. Safe and sound for now. And you're not a fucking cop."

"Ever hear of 911, asshole? They're on the way. If I don't kill you, they will." I glanced over my shoulder. The guy was still breathing. "Why'd you shoot him?"

Silence, then, "He tried to reason with me, said I had the wrong people, that someone else killed my brother. He went for his gun."

I wiped my brow. "He didn't have a gun, so you can't claim self-defense. But if you let Nick and Elizabeth go, you might make a case."

More silence, and I wondered whether he was mulling over my dumb self-defense theory. I was afraid of taking a shot, though I had a sense of where Rick was positioned.

"Don't be a coward. I'm here by the door. Mano-a-mano. Come out alone, or will you be standing behind a woman, like your pussy brother?"

He charged out of the room, his eyes wild with rage, and got off three rounds, all over my head. He still had a few left in the chamber.

I pulled off a shot to his leg, and he screamed. I charged and took a hard leap, slamming my gun across his face. He cried out, tried taking me down, but I whacked him twice before he landed against the wall. He brought up his gun hand, but before he had a chance, I pulled off three rounds, two in the chest and one in his gun arm, which now dropped out of action. He gazed up at me as I kicked away his weapon.

"Fuck you."

His last words.

I waited a moment. "It's okay to come out."

Nick and Elizabeth stood at the bedroom door. Nick looked down at Rick, then shifted to the other male. He froze.

I'd forgotten about the other guy and rushed over to him. I looked down and noticed a large scar down his cheek.

I turned to Nick. "Chance?"

He remained still and nodded.

My guardian angel. "Where the hell are the paramedics?" I demanded. I feared losing another person and dialed for help one more time.

"He's still breathing!" I rushed to stop the bleeding.

Nick knelt beside Chance and took his hand.

His unfocused eyes glazed up at Nick. "So sorry."

"It's okay, friend. I forgive you."

Chance attempted to smile, but his mouth drooped.

"Hang in there, buddy." This from Nick.

The paramedics arrived, along with a few uniforms, one I recognized from Terry's murder. I pushed to my feet and wearily gave him the details. "Detective Walker should be notified."

Nick stood back, watching the team work on Chance. He was crying softly. Elizabeth held him and cried too, probably for her sister.

After the medics carried Chance away, I counted the number of deaths or murders I'd been a part of over the past week. It was a record for me, and I hoped I didn't have to add Chance to my list.

My cell buzzed. Walker.

"I'll be there in five minutes. I expect an explanation."

I glanced around the crime scene. "There's a lot to talk about."

He then told me when this was over, he expected me to go home, before Fort Lauderdale became a battleground.

I think he was kidding.

THIRTY-NINE

In spite of Detective Walker strongly suggesting I leave Fort Lauderdale, maybe for good, I decided to stick around a few days. I needed a vacation, and what better way to spend it than on the beach?

I also wanted to assure Nick and Elizabeth, who were still traumatized by recent events, that I was available for anything, including hand-holding and assuring them their future was bright.

Elizabeth never dreamed Amanda would take over the carwash with Sammy, no less. Eager to start fresh with Nick, she vowed to sell it to the highest bidder, no matter the price.

Ah, Nick. He almost lost his mind, but he survived, as did Chance. He would remain in the hospital for at least a month, but it appeared a full recovery was expected.

This came from Nick, who had just visited him. We talked about Chance at a local bar—not Courtney's. Nick wanted to discuss how Chance had saved them from Rick.

He took a long gulp from his beer. "I discovered Chance and my wife were having an affair the same way most people get caught. They were careless and sloppy, sending text messages back and forth. I happened to see one on my wife's phone. They were going to meet at a local motel, off a main drag. Why they didn't just hang out at Chance's place, I had no idea. Maybe to make it more romantic being on neutral territory."

He stopped, caught his breath. "I can't believe I'm telling you this. Anyway, I watched as she walked into the lobby, all smiles. I was both confused and angry; Chance was my best friend. I left in a rage, and when she returned home all happy, I asked where she'd been.

'With the girls,' she said and told me she was tired and ready to go to sleep."

Nick took a sip of his drink then stared into his glass.

I could tell by his sad expression it was still a raw subject.

He continued. "I followed them a few more times, all ending at the same motel. The last time was different. They met at a bar and stayed over an hour while I waited outside like an idiot. When they left, I could see they were tipsy and got in my wife's car. Chance drove. The night had been rainy, and it suddenly got worse."

Nick stopped as though he was about to become confessional. His eyes met mine. "I'm not happy about what I did, but I was jealous and out of my mind. I felt so betrayed by both of them."

I nodded for him to continue.

"I followed them, but the rain kept falling hard, and I could see Chance's driving was erratic. I could have turned and gone home, but my rage compelled me to follow them."

He paused. "It was a lonely road—we still have a few in South Florida, and I put on my high beams. I kept flashing, and he must have gotten spooked, because he picked up his speed and left me where I could barely make out his taillights."

Nick stopped, downed his drink, and peered inside the glass. He looked over at me. "I killed her and the baby."

I attempted to hold back my surprise, but Nick must have noticed my dread expression.

"I know, it's bad, and I never told anyone this, but, after all that's happened, I need to come forward. My guilt hasn't subsided since that night. Between that and my patient dying, I flipped out."

"You said you killed her. I'm not hearing that yet, but I'm not asking as a cop, but a friend. How?"

Nick held off a moment, swallowed hard. "If I hadn't... chased them, Chance wouldn't have crashed the car. It's that simple."

Simple, it wasn't.

"Did they know you were tailing them?"

"Know?" He shook his head. "I don't believe so. But that's not the point, Hank. I had a hand in...their deaths."

"Your wife and child?"

Nick scowled. *"Their* child. I'm infertile!" He stopped, composed himself. "I pushed Chance to speed up, and with the ground wet, he slammed into a tree."

Visions of Amanda. I sighed, then asked, "Did you call for help?"

He shut his eyes, and when he opened them, tears formed. "I couldn't. I know I should have, but the police would've known it was me. How would it look? My wife and lover in one car and me following. I've been dealing with that mistake ever since." A long sigh.

"But the police called you after the accident, right?"

"Yes, of course. They told me my wife and the baby died instantly. Chance was barely alive at the hospital. I didn't visit him, and he was still in the hospital the day of the funeral."

Nick called over the bartender and ordered another round.

"That was the hard part. Having a funeral for my wife and their child. He would have been born a boy had he lived."

Nick was still angry. "And Chance, have you seen him since the accident? I mean before today?"

Nick shook his head in a daze. "He tried, but I told him to go to hell with my wife. That was the last time until…now. Funny, after all that, he saved my life. Elizabeth's and mine."

"If it'll make you feel better, Chance was the main reason we were able to solve the case." I told Nick about my phantom text guy. "I don't know how he did it, but if it wasn't for him…"

Nick smiled thinly. "Chance is a cyber security geek. He owns a company that works with law enforcement. Highly secretive. Even I don't know the extent of his capabilities. He told me today he had me covered—and you, Hank."

I thought of the motorist who stopped at the crash site and realized Chance couldn't have been two places at once. He must have sent one of his—geeks.

Made sense.

"I should have asked him to put a tail on my wife." He laughed sadly. "Right."

Another round of drinks arrived.

Nick looked down at his drink.

"What?" I asked.

"I don't understand how Chance just showed up after all these months."

"Maybe he was following the news and saw what was happening to you."

Nick nodded. "Maybe."

"He must have known you were being set up." I shrugged. "Whatever it was that prompted him, I'm grateful."

"Me too." He smiled warmly.

I asked, "That day in your apartment when Chance was shot, Rick said Chance tried talking him down, but obviously, that didn't happen."

Nick nodded. "Chance attempted the impossible. He arrived

soon after Rick accosted Elizabeth and me outside my building. He had a gun pointed at my back. Elizabeth knew him, of course. She was his sister-in-law. When we arrived at my apartment, he pushed us into the living room and accused us of killing his brother. Said we would pay."

He took another sip, then another. "Elizabeth swore we had nothing to do with it and blamed Amanda."

"She said that?" I asked, lifting my beer bottle.

"She had no choice. Besides, it was true. Anyway, that pissed Rick off even more. He was tired of the twins' blame game. He told us he grabbed Amanda in her house, who swore it wasn't her. Only, at the time, he was talking to Elizabeth."

I mentioned discovering Elizabeth in the trunk of the car inside Amanda's garage.

"Rick admitted it was him. She would have died if you hadn't found her, Hank."

"Or Rick would've returned and killed her," I added.

"At that point, Rick grew agitated, so when Chance arrived and tried talking him out of killing us, he lost it and shot Chance."

Nick bowed his head. "It was so quick. Rick must have realized what he had gotten himself into and pushed us into the bedroom. He kept mumbling stuff; I have no idea what, but we were afraid he'd shoot us too."

Nick met my eyes. "And then you showed up. You saved us from that maniac, Hank. We wouldn't be alive if it wasn't for you." He touched my shoulder. "Thank you."

I smiled briefly. I looked around the empty bar and realized the time. I was ready to head back to my hotel, but I had one more question.

"How is it that you and Elizabeth connected so quickly after only one night, especially when she disappeared the following morning? It sounded like a one-night stand."

He smiled. "Kismet, perhaps. There was something special about the evening, and I'm not just talking sex—which was great. I felt we had become one person. Elizabeth felt the same. I hadn't connected with another person like that. Ever. Not even with my wife. I wasn't willing to give her up. The disturbing phone call that morning, the one I thought was a prank, well, I realized it wasn't. I sensed Elizabeth was in danger, and I had to act."

"And you called JR."

"And he immediately thought of you. Said you were the best."

"You're making me blush," I teased.

"He was right. You're the reason Elizabeth and I have another chance."

"Right, *Chance.*"

He smiled sadly. "Enough of the past. I'm ready to go forward, forgive and renew my relationship with him. I know he feels the same. He told me so when I visited him in the hospital. He's making progress."

Nick stopped and smiled.

"What?"

"Chance told me you did a great job. Says he wants to offer you a position with his company."

I laughed. "I kind of like it where I am right now, though I'd die for Fort Lauderdale in the winter."

"Who wouldn't? Think about it, Hank."

Nick and I parted ways, maybe for the last time. Hopefully, he and Elizabeth would have that second chance. That was what we all hoped for.

The End

BRIDGE TO MURDER

A HANK REED MYSTERY, BOOK 4

June 29, 1995

Whitestone, New York

Luca Caruso entered the family living room, not quite ready to leave for his birthday bash. He glanced over at his mother, an attractive woman in her forties with short dark brown hair and a wistful smile, as she sat comfortably on the sofa reading a romance novel.

"I guess I should be heading out," Luca said. "It's almost seven."

She peered up from her book. "You behave yourself tonight, young man. I know you're eighteen, but don't get crazy and drink yourself silly or fall in the river. Now, give me a hug and kiss."

Ever since his father had been murdered five years before, Luca's mother had become overprotective. And he let her voice her concern. She loved him.

Luca wasn't worried about falling in the East River. He was

concerned about surviving the night, which had nothing to do with drinking.

"Promise," he said. He gave her a long hug, then sighed. He wanted to hold on forever, but that wasn't possible, at least not until he settled the situation. If he settled it. The night would tell.

Luca turned and grabbed a flashlight off the end table. A bottle of Russian vodka was waiting for him on the stoop.

He turned back to her from the door. "I love you, Mom."

She smiled tenderly. "That's sweet. I love you too, son. Now go and have a good time, Whitestone Boy."

Luca closed the door, picked up the vodka, which was inside a paper bag, and hustled down the block. The Whitestone Bridge stood a few blocks away, a full moon shining on the festive cable necklace bridge lights with a mirror image on the tranquil East River.

He was now less than a block from Francis Lewis Park (renamed from the Whitestone Park), where the giant boulder called Hells Bells stood like a sentry, a hundred feet in the water. On warm days, the boys would swim out to the monstrous mass and cautiously climb to the top, like their fathers before them. Rumor had it someone stood on top and yelled out Hell's Bells. The name stuck.

Swimming out to Hells Bells wasn't on the boys' agenda that night, drinking and partying was. Luca, the youngest of the five Whitestone Boys, as they called themselves, had just turned eighteen.

His visions turned dark, very dark, as he heard his friends chatting amongst themselves. Luca couldn't wait until this night was over, and he was back in his kitchen with his mother and sister, Lisa, eating and chatting away about his night with the boys. At least, he hoped his story would end on a high note.

"Hey," he called out to his buddies, his voice off.

"Finally, the king has arrived." Matt Larkin, Luca's best friend, bowed to him.

"You don't sound too enthusiastic," slurred Jesse. The cap to his Bacardi rum bottle unscrewed. "Can't wait forever."

Kyle and Alex grinned and raised their drinks.

"Let's party." Matt led the way, past the park and onto the dirt path leading under the bridge, flashlight in hand, a bright beam piercing the way.

The bridge landing was theirs for the night. Normally, the spot was a sanctuary where fishermen turned inward and thought of life while casting for a complying fish, where lovers took chances, and where an occasional fight broke out. Not tonight. The boys were alone, as though they had reserved the area for themselves.

Luca sat on the edge of a boulder, quietly taking in the fun. His friends were getting silly and wasted, which was good, because he needed them asleep when he left. His heart sank at the thought of never seeing them again, and so he took a mental snapshot of the group. He imagined their future: married with kids. He wanted that, too, with Tara. He just needed to get past tonight.

One by one, the boys began curling up on the dirt. It was after two in the morning, and Luca had a few hours to get to his destination. He waited another half-hour, alone in his thoughts. He then stood over each one, and when he was certain they'd be out for hours, he made his move.

He jogged and reached Fort Totten Park by four a.m. The military tunnel, which had been used during the Civil War, was where he and the Whitestone Boys had spent afternoons inside hanging out, smoking cigarettes, and telling scary stories.

Luca kept vacillating about his options: fight or flight. He knew fighting would be senseless, but maybe he could talk his way out of his predicament. He'd been a good debater at Flushing High School.

God, he wished his father were still around to protect him. He'd been a minor player for the Mob and was killed in the line of screwing up. Maybe Luca should have told Bobby, his mother's cop boyfriend, about the situation. Surely, he could do something. He turned around to the parking lot and sighed. A little too late for that.

Dad, why did they kill you?

As five a.m. arrived, so did the enemy. He watched as a car's high beams streamed into the park. Oh, God! Luca looked back at the tunnel one more time and said a short prayer.

Either way, he'd be ready.

Available in Paperback and eBook from Your Favorite Bookstore or Online Retailer

ACKNOWLEDGMENTS

This has been a trying time for everyone, writers included—no thanks to the Coronavirus. The love and support I've received from family and friends to keep pushing helped me enormously. I pushed through, and the result became my third Hank Reed thriller, The Edge of Murder.

Thanks to my writer group, particularly over the past six months, when our critiques were channeled and limited to email. Thanks to Sharon and George and to my editor, Lacie Redding, who guided me throughout.

Thanks go out to my advanced readers, Sonia Lichtenberg, Derek Taylor, and Peg Kelly, along with my mental health advisers, Mark Lichtenberg, as well as Marla Berger and my publisher at ePublishing Works!, Brian Paules and his staff.

My gratitude goes to my law enforcement friends Bob Marchant and Al Hallonquist, and my legal adviser, Bill Berger.

Thanks to all!

ABOUT THE AUTHOR

Fred Lichtenberg is a native New Yorker who resides with his wife in Jupiter, Florida. He has one son. After spending a career as a Field Agent with the IRS, Lichtenberg changed gears from crunching numbers to creating fictitious villains and heroes. *Hunter's World* (currently titled The Art of Murder), the first book in the Hank Reed Series, begins with the murder of an outside celebrity living in a small community on Long Island. Lichtenberg's second book, *Murder on the Rocks,* takes Hank Reed (now a Suffolk County Detective) in search of a missing person presumably involved in a whistleblower investigation.

The Edge of Murder shifts Hank from a detective to a private investigator, where he searches for a missing woman.

Lichtenberg's stand-alone novels include: *Double Trouble; Deadly Heat at The Cottages: Sex, Murder, and Mayhem; Murder 1040: The Final Audit;* and the humorous, *Retired: Now What?*

Lichtenberg also wrote *The Second Time Around...Again,* a one-act play about finding love in a nursing home, performed at the Lake Worth Playhouse.

Fred is an active member of the Mystery Writers of America and International Thriller Writers.

www.fredlichtenberg.com

facebook.com/fredlichtenberg